FROM A VIEW TO A DEATH

ANTHONY POWELL was born in London in 1905. His father was a soldier, of a family mostly soldiers or sailors, which moved from Wales about a hundred and fifty years ago. He was educated at Eton and Balliol College, Oxford, of which he is now an Honorary Fellow.

From 1926 he worked for about nine years at Duckworths, the publishers, then as scriptwriter for Warner Brothers in England. During the war he served in the Welch Regiment and Intelligence Corps; acting as Liaison Officer with the Polish, Belgian, Czechoslovak, Free French and Luxembourg forces, and being promoted major.

Before and after World War II he wrote reviews and literary columns for various papers, including the *Daily Telegraph* and the *Spectator*. From 1948-52 he worked on the *Times Literary Supplement*, and was Literary Editor of *Punch*, 1952-58.

Between 1931 and 1949, Anthony Powell published five novels, a biography, *John Aubrey and His Friends*, and a selection from Aubrey's works. The first volume of his twelve-volume novel, *A Dance to the Music of Time*, was published in 1951, and the concluding volume, *Hearing Secret Harmonies*, appeared in 1975. In 1976 he published the first volume of his memoirs, *To Keep the Ball Rolling*, under the title *Infants of the Spring*.

In 1934 he married Lady Violet Pakenham, daughter of the fifth Earl of Longford. They have two sons. They live in Somerset, to which they moved in 1952.

Books by Anthony Powell

NOVELS
Afternoon Men
Venusberg
Agents and Patients
What's Become of Waring

A DANCE TO THE MUSIC OF TIME
A Question of Upbringing
A Buyer's Market
The Acceptance World
At Lady Molly's
Casanova's Chinese Restaurant
The Kindly Ones
The Valley of Bones
The Soldier's Art
The Military Philosophers
Books Do Furnish a Room
Temporary Kings
Hearing Secret Harmonies

TO KEEP THE BALL ROLLING (MEMOIRS)
Volume I: Infants of the Spring

GENERAL
John Aubrey and His Friends

PLAYS
The Garden God *and* The Rest I'll Whistle

ANTHONY POWELL

From a View to a Death

FONTANA BOOKS
BY AGREEMENT WITH
HEINEMANN

First published in 1933 by Gerald Duckworth & Co Ltd
First issued in Fontana Books 1968
Second Impression February 1979

Made and printed in Great Britain by
William Collins Sons & Co Ltd, Glasgow

"From a drag to a chase, from a chase to a view,
From a view to a death in the morning."

John Peel

ONE

They drove uncertainly along the avenue that led to the house, through the bars of light that fell between the tree-trunks and made the shadows of the lime-trees strike obliquely across the gravel. The navy-blue car was built high off the ground and the name on its bonnet recalled a bank-rupt, forgotten firm of motor-makers. Inside, the car was done up in a material like grey corduroy, with folding seats in unexpected places, constructed liberally to accommodate some Edwardian Swiss Family Robinson. This was a period piece. An exhibit. The brakes had ceased to work long since. On the wall in front, immediately behind the chauffeur's neck, which was goose-flesh in spite of the heat, there was a German silver vase for flowers and below it a looking-glass, distorting but powerful. In this Zouch examined his face, wondering what sort of an impression he would make when he arrived. Not too good a one, he felt, if the mirror was to be relied upon. He sat on the edge of the grey upholstery, leaning forward, trying to discount the elongating tendency of the glass and the havoc that it played with his beard. Twenty-nine next year, he thought. The V comprised by the lapels of his coat and enclosing his shirt, collar and tie was all right. It had that touch of ingenuousness that was expected of a painter. His shoes, vast golfing brogues with hobnails, were all right too. It was the beard that he was least certain about, but it had served him well in the past and he saw no reason why it should not do so again. He lay back stiffly—it was impossible to loll in these seats—feeling as if he were sitting in the lounge of a small

French hotel, which the car's interior resembled in size and taste.

Describing a semicircle and grinding up the drive in front of the portico, they stopped with a jerk at the entrance to the house. Zouch got out. He took the several canvases that he had brought with him and held them under his arm, leaving the rest of his luggage for the chauffeur to look after. Then he went up the steps. He put out his hand to ring the bell, but before he could do this the door was opened by a butler, a thin-lipped jesuitical man with a stern, sad face. Holding the canvases under one arm and the mackintosh over the other, Zouch muttered thickly to himself. There seemed no alternative method of approach.

"Mr. Zouch, sir?"

"Yes."

"The young ladies," said the butler, with just the hint of a threat in his voice, "are on the lawn."

He stood in front of Zouch as if he thought that it might be unsafe to allow him to walk unaccompanied through the house but at the same time was unwilling personally to escort him to its occupants. Zouch side-stepped and put down the canvases and the mackintosh on an oak chest, already covered with hats and gloves and dog-whips. The butler swung round, on the look-out.

"Is the lawn straight through?"

"Straight through, sir."

"Then I expect I shall be able to find them."

"Very good, sir."

He walked towards the room opposite, away from the butler, who seemed now turned to stone. Through an open door he could see french windows, which allowed a narrow shaft of yellow sun to fall in the hall and throw up a highlight from the floorboards on to a picture. There were several pictures on the walls. Wide smoky landscapes, copies of copies of romantically conceived Italian ruins. He noticed that the hall had a smell of its own, partly furniture polish, partly the fragrance of rose-petals. This was a house with a robust flavour. He moved on, one of the hobnails of his shoe skidding on the parquet. The butler, as if waiting for his Pygmalion, made no effort to follow but stood stock still, seeming to consider whether or not to throw back Zouch's suitcase on to the drive. Zouch pressed forward and gained the morning-room, which was lighter than the hall and hung with engravings. Someone was sitting reading a newspaper in the far corner of the room, but pretending that he did not see this person and quickening his pace, he reached the windows unaccosted and passed through and out into the thundery sunshine. Placidly the garden stretched away in front of him.

The lawn came up close to the house and sloped away for some distance until it reached trees and a piece of artificial water. Beyond this small lake were fields, and the land began to rise again until the criss-cross lines made by the hedges became indistinct. At the back of this expanse of green country were low hills, cut out neatly as if in cardboard. Down by the water there was a croquet lawn, on which two girls stood talking. He saw that one of them was Mary Passenger. She was standing with her back to him, leaning on her mallet and talking to the other girl. He walked towards them, thinking of things to say. As he came near, Mary Passenger turned and, catching sight of him, waved. Zouch approached the croquet lawn circumspectly.

"Hallo," she said, when he was close.

"Hallo, Mary."

"So you got here all right? Dawkin didn't drive you into the ditch? I'm afraid it's a terribly old car."

She was nervous, not used to him yet. Her shyness made

her sound cross. The afternoon sun poured down on to the lawn and Zouch felt himself sweating. He was wearing too thick a suit for the time of year. He said:

"No. There were no accidents of any kind. We came here quite safely all the way from the station."

"Oh, good."

"The car went very well."

There was a pause. To arrive was to die a little. Half-past three in the afternoon was, as always, a difficult time of day to deal with. Mary Passenger tapped the turf with her mallet. She was about twenty-four with good, rather over-emphasised features and an appearance that was almost aggressively healthy. She said:

"But you haven't met my sister yet, have you? Betty, this is Arthur Zouch."

The sister moved forward and they shook hands. Betty Passenger was considerably older than Mary. She had a round and heavily made-up face with a large, engaging mouth. Zouch knew that she had done something in the past which everyone regarded as disgraceful but at that moment he was unable to call to mind what particular action this had been. He said:

"Haven't I seen you somewhere before?"

He thought it better to leave any likely places unspecified.

"Quite possible," she said. "I'm sure I've seen you some-where too. Was it in Paris? The Dôme or the Ritz bar or somewhere like that?"

"Perhaps it was."

"I used to live there. In Paris, I mean."

Mary Passenger listened to them, frowning a little, still knocking her mallet on the ground. It seemed that she pre-ferred that her elder sister should not talk too much. She said to Zouch:

"Would you like to come for a walk before tea?"

"Very much."

"Are you coming, Betty?"

Betty said: "I shall go and have a bath. This is the only time of day that the water is ever hot in this house."

"Betty, you can't."

"Why not?"

"Will you take this back with you then?"

Betty took her sister's mallet as well as her own. She walked away in the direction of the house, dragging the two mallets behind her and humming a little to herself. Mary watched her for a moment or two and then said:

"Come this way. We'll go round by the pond."

They left the lawn and went down a narrow path that led by the water and under the trees. Even here, out of the sun, the air was sultry. There was a heaviness in the atmosphere, and a sickly smell of decayed leaves hung about in this part of the garden. Once or twice Zouch felt a sting in his leg from the insects that were hovering about low off the ground. Everything was very still apart from the buzzing of the insects. A storm was not far away.

"It's so nice that you should have been able to come," Mary said.

She knew very little about this sort of young man and Zouch himself was not yet altogether at his ease. He saw that the first few hours must be spent in renewing contacts such as they were, if any. He might, of course, have made a mistake. That remained to be seen. But somehow he did not think that he had made a mistake. He made very few mistakes of that kind.

"What a lovely place this is," he said.

"It is rather nice, isn't it? But not if you have to live there too long."

"I suppose not."

She looked at him sideways. Zouch smiled at her, as

agreeably as he was able, through his beard. Mary smiled
back at him and lowered her eyes. They went on and out
of the garden and into a park where a few deer were
grazing.

Zouch was a superman. A fair English equivalent of the
Teutonic ideal of the *Übermensch*. No one knew this yet
except himself. That was because he had not been one long
enough for people to find out. They would learn all in good
time; and to their cost. Meanwhile he went on his way,
taking but not giving, treating life as a sort of quick-lunch
counter where you helped yourself and all the snacks were
free. He was ambitious, naturally, and painted bright, lifeless portraits that would have been hung in the Academy if
he had sent them there but which he preferred to show in
smaller galleries having the reputation for being modern.
His preponderance therefore lay in the spheres, stressed by
English educationalists, of character rather than developed
talent. He had some skill in catching a likeness, and this,
combined with a simple colour formula and an instinct for
saying the sort of thing that sitters expected of a painter,
caused him to be spoken of as promising. Although, as it
happened, he was short of money at the moment, his work
had already begun to bring him in a comfortable income
and his parents, who kept a bookshop in a north country
town and who had never succeeded in throwing off wholly
the influence of William Morris, thought the world of him.
He was good-looking, too, on a small scale, and rather in
spite of his short fair beard. He liked women but never put
them before his work. The women whom he liked were at
present the only persons who guessed at all that they were
dealing with a superman.

His life had not been too easy at the start. But this was
a strength to him because it had left him with a contempt

both for persons who had themselves had no early struggles and also for those who found themselves compelled to continue struggling in later life. For some years now things had gone well with him, but just when he had decided to move into a bigger studio and to begin forging ahead in earnest, three important patrons, two dowagers and a rich old man, had died unexpectedly, and the gallery where his summer show had been held went into liquidation and its proprietor removed to a mental home. All this showed him how careful one had to be. The Passengers' invitation was in these circumstances timely. He hoped to prolong his visit to all reasonable limits. In the winter, when people came back to London, things might look up a bit. Meanwhile, he thought, the policy was to sit tight.

He had seen Mary Passenger for the first time only a few months before, at the house of a woman whose portrait he was painting. Mary was shown in by mistake by the maid, who had orders to say that her mistress was out. They were introduced to each other and at once, rather surprisingly, got on very well together, to the displeasure of their hostess. Mary, who had by that time spent several years of her life in going to dances, staying in house-parties, watching shooting in Scotland and taking part in hunting in England, thought herself a little tired of these aspects of life. No immediate alternative offered itself to her imagination but she had already begun to occupy herself by reading a great many novels, and when she met Zouch she liked him because he talked to her about persons who earned their living by writing or painting, and in this way he represented to her a world with which she had no first-hand contacts. She was not really interested in these subjects, but then for that matter neither was Zouch, and it made a change for her while he, in return, found her attractive. He also saw at once that a little conversation would add a country

house to his week-ending list. At the very beginning of his
career he had become aware of the importance of looking
ahead.

The Passengers were not rich. For several generations
none of them had had any clear idea of how to manage their
business affairs and the family had become accustomed to
having less and less money as the years went on. But at the
period when this financial maladroitness had set in they had
owned some valuable property, so that even now they re-
tained enough to keep up Passenger Court and a house near
Belgrave Square, barely habitable on account of its
draughts. The *mariages de convenance* of an earlier generation had left them related, even if distantly, to almost
everyone of any importance in the world in which they
lived, so that things might have been worse, but Mary's
father had been at pains to antagonise so many of his own
and his wife's relations that the unfortunate marriage of
his elder daughter, Betty, was regarded by many substantial
observers as a direct judgment on him. The only redeeming
feature of Betty's marriage was that it had left her with
the title of "duchess" and, although the Passenger family
themselves had been always, and remained always, unim-
pressed by this, even they were forced to admit that among
the less sophisticated (but for that reason not necessarily less
influential) elements in the county, the title was regarded
as an ameliorating circumstance. Sometimes a new house-
maid would refer to her in the presence of the wincing Mr.
Passenger as "Her Grace" instead of "Miss Betty", but the
family laughed it off somehow and Betty herself was
quite indifferent to whatever style she went under. It was
hoped that Mary, whose tastes in early life seemed simple
enough, would make a marriage that would prove a glowing contrast to her sister's disagreeable Italian alliance, the

crowning annoyance of which had been that Betty had been left with a daughter.

The Passengers had lived at Passenger Court for about a hundred and fifty years but, as the house had been burnt down twice and rebuilt in the late nineteenth century in imitation "Georgian", their seat was of no great architectural interest. But it was a comfortable house to stay in because Mrs. Passenger was herself quite fond of food, and her husband, in spite of his shortcomings, rarely hung about after meals to embarrass his daughters' guests.

Leaving the park, Mary and Zouch struck across the fields to make a detour that would bring them at the end of their walk to the other side of the garden. Conversationally, Zouch was getting back into his stride and he knew that by the evening he would be in good form. At the same time Mary was becoming more accustomed to him. They climbed over a gate leading into a green road marked by cart-ruts. Along the other side of this road there were gorse bushes and a low hedge. As he jumped down from the gate Zouch heard someone shout to them and, looking up the road, he saw an extravagantly stylised figure break through the bracken farther up the lane and jump the ditch. It was an elderly man who had shouted and who carried in his appearance something other-worldly and strange. He had a white moustache and was dressed in check riding-breeches, gaiters, a coat with two slits up the back, and a brown hat with several fishing-flies stuck into the band. He had the air of a legendary creature of the woods, Herne the Hunter almost, with a touch of the romantic gamekeeper, some Lady Chatterley's superannuated lover, and yet at the same time he looked more of a country gentleman than perhaps any country gentleman could ever hope to look. He was followed by a spaniel of low descent.

"Out for a walk?" he shouted again, coming up close to them.

"Yes," said Mary. "A walk before tea. This is Mr. Zouch. I don't think you have met Major Fosdick."

"What's his name?"

"Zouch."

"Come down for the pageant, has he?" said Major Fosdick.

Moistly, he peered at Zouch. The skin of his face was covered with small diagonal lines, similar in pattern to those on his coat. Mary said:

"Well, he hasn't been told about it yet, but he will certainly be expected to take part."

"We want everybody we can get. Everybody."

"Oh yes," said Mary, "I'm going to get everybody I can."

Major Fosdick's face, blotchy in places, worked up and down convulsively as if he were chewing gum, his dewlaps giving him something of the appearance of a bloodhound. He said:

"I've just been round to see your father. About North Copse, you know. After all the place is wedge shaped, and if a few birds do sometimes come across I can't help it, can I?"

"It's all rather difficult, I know."

"It's a bottle-neck," said the Major, as if this excused any eccentricities of conduct on his part.

"Yes, I suppose it is."

"But we've got things all shipshape now."

"You have?"

Major Fosdick laughed throatily and then stopped laughing all of a sudden, as if he thought he had gone too far. He coughed several times and cleared his throat and laughed again, but irresolutely this time. His dog, all

at once overcome by the heat, lay on the ground as if dead.
Major Fosdick said:

"Well, I suppose I shall have to be getting along now.
Thought I'd like a bit of exercise before tea."

"Good-bye," said Mary.

"Rehearsal on Thursday, don't forget."

"We won't forget."

"Good-bye. Good-bye."

Major Fosdick walked away at a smart pace, the mustard-
coloured dog rising with difficulty and following at heel.
They watched him turn the corner of the road and dis-
appear. Mary fanned herself with a dock-leaf which she
had picked while talking to the Major. She said:

"I suppose we ought to be getting back now too."

"Who was that? He must be very hot in those clothes."

"He's called Major Fosdick. They live about two miles
from here, on the edge of the town. He's got two sons.
You're sure to meet them while you're down here."

"What are they like?"

Mary looked at him half-uncomprehendingly. She had
not yet advanced so far as to know what people were like.
Anyway she had no language in which to describe them to
Zouch. She said:

"Oh, I don't know. One of them was in the war. The
other is at Oxford. He's rather odd."

"In what way?"

Mary was at a loss.

"He's just odd," she said.

They turned back in the direction of the park. The hot
sky had made a deep blue rim along the horizon in front of
them. In the wood near-by a bird was singing shrilly as
if it were spring and not late summer.

Major Fosdick, followed by his plebeian spaniel, continued in the direction of his home. They debouched together from the green lane on to the main road, both narrowly escaping death from a Brobdingnagian bus, lumbering towards the town at fifty miles an hour on the wrong side of the road. Wholly enveloped in the cloud of dust and petrol-fumes left in its trail, more than ever like a spectre conjured up out of the mist, the Major tramped along, crunching down the small stones that had been scattered over the tar.

Major Fosdick was thinking that he had told that fellow Passenger what was what. Just because he lived in a big house that was no reason why he should imagine that he owned every bird in the county. The sun flickered over the pronounced pattern of the Major's coat and lit up the elbows, which had been reinforced with leather.

He was reaching the outskirts of the town now and he could see his own house only a few hundred yards off. It was a small house and stood a little way back from the road, and there were posts along the front of it connected by chains. Major Fosdick, who had seen the façade many times before from this aspect, still wished that he could afford something larger. He was about to pass between the posts and enter his house when he noticed that Joanna Brandon was coming up the street towards him. It was proving an eventful afternoon.

"Hallo, Joanna," he shouted.

Joanna advanced in his direction, making a noncommittal gesture at him with the dog-whip she carried. She was followed by two dropsical mongrels like monstrously swollen caterpillars, who were soon snuffling and grunting round the Major's dog, bent on picking, if possible, a quarrel.

"Out for a walk?"

"Yes," said Joanna, "I've been taking the dogs for a run."

She was a thin girl, about the same age as Mary Passenger.

"Dogs want plenty of exercise," said Major Fosdick. He watched Joanna's dogs without approval and stirred one of them with his stick.

"They come out with me every afternoon. I usually have nothing else to do."

"Why not drop in and have some tea?" said the Major. He was not particularly interested in how Joanna spent her afternoons, but he had a weakness for young girls and admired the way she carried herself.

"It's just about tea-time," he said.

"I can't. I must get back and see how mother is getting on."

"Yes, yes. Of course. I've just been up to see Vernon Passenger. About North Copse, you know."

"Oh, have you?"

"It's a wedge."

"Is it?" said Joanna, who had no idea what the Major was talking about and cared less.

"He took it all in very good part," said Major Fosdick, implying that the interview had ended in physical violence. "He knows as well as I do that it's not my fault if a few of his birds come over. It's a bottle-neck. On the way back I met Mary Passenger and a young man who is staying up there with them. A young fellow with a beard."

"Did you?"

"I had a few words with them about the pageant. You're coming to the rehearsal on Thursday, of course?"

"Oh yes. Of course."

"We must get everybody we can. People are bound to drop out at the last moment."

"They always do, don't they?"

"Well, I suppose I must be getting on now if you really won't come in and have some tea."

"No really, thanks. Good-bye."

"Good-bye, Joanna."

She waved her whip and once more Major Fosdick advanced between the posts. The front door was ajar and he walked through and, opening the inner door, he hung his hat on one of the massive hooks of the mahogany umbrella-stand. Then he went into the drawing-room, a small room packed with furniture, the walls of which were entirely covered with landscapes in water-colour, executed by his wife. His two sons, Jasper and Torquil, were sitting at tea. Major Fosdick hardly saw them. He was so used to their being there and to their looking exactly as they looked at that moment that he noticed them no more than he noticed the horsehair settee in the middle of the room or the gnu's head in the hall.

The names of the Fosdick sons had been in the Fosdick family for several generations and were not therefore in themselves any indication of personal eccentricity. On the contrary, it was in this case the names which took on a vicarious importance from their owners rather than the reverse and, on the whole, more probable process. Jasper was the elder and the one who had been in the army. He was tall and seemed to be all knees and elbows and his ears stuck out like outstretched wings on either side of his head. He wore a small moustache of clipped ginger hair of coarse quality and his mouth was usually a little open, hinting of adenoids. He had had several jobs since the Armistice. Nine, to be exact. That was in the first three years after the war. By that time it became clear that he was unsuited to the sort of job that was available. However, at the moment he had prospects because he had been promised the secretaryship of the local golf club when that post fell vacant and that might be soon, because the present secretary was known to have a weak heart. Meanwhile Jasper lived at home and practised short approach shots.

Torquil, on the other hand, was at Oxford. He had been begotten by his parents in a completely different mood from that which had resulted in Jasper. Torquil was small and dark and hungry-looking, with an enormous head that looked as if it might snap off at any moment and fall from his shoulders. He was dressed in the prevailing Oxford fashion of a saffron-coloured high-necked jumper and dove-grey flannel trousers. But in spite of this he was a serious young man who intended to make a career for himself. Somebody had suggested the Church. He himself favoured the Bar.

Mrs. Fosdick was not in the room. She had finished her tea and she was in the garden, picking flowers for the dinner-table. Major Fosdick was as unaware of her absence as he was of the presence of his sons. He took a scone, the only remaining one, from the dish and put it whole into his mouth. When he had swallowed it he said:

"I suppose you two boys know that there is a rehearsal of the pageant on Thursday?"

Jasper said: "Oh yes, rather."

That conversation came to an end. Major Fosdick went on to walnut cake. He was not entertained by either of his sons. He was scarcely aware that the other two persons in the room were his sons. He said:

"I went up and saw old Passenger about North Copse this afternoon. Of course he climbed down at once. There was nothing else for him to do."

Torquil had begun to smoke a cigarette. He smoked it with a short intake of breath, expelling the smoke abruptly in little puffs, as if he were spitting flies from his lip. Major Fosdick said:

"I met Mary Passenger on the way back. They've got a young man staying up there. With a beard."

Jasper, who had begun to read the paper, gave a sudden cackle of laughter at this piece of information, but did not look up. Torquil puffed out a little eddy of smoke and, almost interested, said:

"Is he going to be in the pageant?"

"I suppose so," said his father, trying to make up his mind if he would eat another slice of walnut cake or whether that would spoil his dinner.

Jasper returned to the sports page of his paper, making surprised whistling noises at intervals as he read of startling athletic achievements. At last he threw the newspaper on the floor and, getting up, he put his hands in his pockets and said:

"I think I'll barge along and call on Joanna and ask her if she'd like to come in for a spot of badminton next week."

Major Fosdick said: "I don't think I should go now if I were you, as I spoke to her just before coming in here and she said that she had to go back to her mother. I suggested that she should come and have tea here but she wouldn't come."

"I might barge over just the same. If she's out I'll look up young Kittermaster and we might do some putting on their lawn."

Major Fosdick did not answer. He was thinking of other things. Torquil finished his cigarette and threw it into the fireplace. He said in his high-pitched voice:

"Jasper, do you think if I gave a cocktail party at the Fox and Hounds that I could get the Orphans to come and play?"

Jasper collapsed into his arm-chair again and, in a tremendously energetic piece of overacting, he began to shake with simulated laughter. Major Fosdick finished his second piece of cake. He sat for a few minutes, thinking. Then he got up from his chair and walked slowly out of the room. He had had enough of his sons for the moment. This was his hour. The time to please himself. A period of mental relaxation.

He went upstairs to his dressing-room and when he had arrived there he locked the door. Then he turned to the bottom drawer of his wardrobe, where he kept all his oldest shooting-suits. He knelt down in front of this and pulled it open. Below the piles of tweed was a piece of brown paper and from under the brown paper he took two parcels tied up with string. Major Fosdick undid the loose knots of the first parcel and took from out of it a large picture-hat that had no doubt been seen at Ascot some twenty years before. The second parcel contained a black sequin evening dress of about the same date. Removing his coat and waistcoat, Major Fosdick slipped the evening dress over his head and, shaking it so that it fell down into position, he went to the looking-glass and put on the hat. When he had it arranged at an angle that was to his satisfaction, he lit his pipe and, taking a copy of *Through the Western Highlands with Rod and Gun* from the dressing-table, he sat down. In this costume he read until it was time to change for dinner.

For a good many years now he had found it restful to do this for an hour or two every day when he had the opportunity. He himself would have found it difficult to account for such an eccentricity to anyone whom he might have happened to encounter during one of these periods and it was for this reason that he was accustomed to gratify his whim only at times when there was a reasonable expectation that his privacy would be respected by his family. Publicly he himself would refer to these temporary retirements from the arena of everyday life as his Forty Winks.

Relieved at her success in having avoided the *longueurs* of tea at the Fosdicks', Joanna whistled to the dogs and set out in the direction of home. It was an escape. On an afternoon as hot as this one, tea at the Fosdicks' was not to be thought of. One of the reasons against it was that Jasper Fosdick was in love with her. He had been in love with her in a heavy, dumb-animal sort of way almost as long as she could remember. At least, it seemed as long as that to Joanna. She could imagine how solicitous he would have been, in spite of the heat, if she had accepted his father's invitation. She did not care for Jasper. She preferred Torquil, if a choice had to be made. She walked across the cobbled market-place, past the war memorial, and went up a side turning.

As was usual at this time of day, the Orphans were at the corner of the street with their organ. The bright sunlight splashed against the sweat of their faces and the patent-leather peaks of the yachting caps that they wore. Their organ was playing *Les Cloches de Corneville*, and they were taking it in turns to work the handle, the unoccupied pair making it their business to importune, when it occurred to them to do so, anyone who passed by and at other times, when the street was empty, to twitch and grumble at each other. There was a notice in front of the organ which said *Friend, Spare a Penny for us, Orphans of this Town*. That was all. There was no appeal to patriotism except of a purely local sort and there was no recital of past achievements, military or otherwise, which might rationally be supposed to carry with them a right to the gratitude of the nation at large. On the contrary the postulation rested wholly on the handicap of loss of parents, which because the youngest of the Orphans must have been at least forty years of age, was in their case presumed to have persisted into early middle life. The three of them had small round heads and beady half-closed eyes. Hair grew on their faces but not successfully. It was sporadic, and in the case of one of the Orphans only was it of sufficient density to form a moustache. Nor was this entirely satisfactory as a feature on account of its colour and unpleasant texture, recalling in this respect Jasper Fosdick's upper lip.

Joanna crossed to the other side of the street when she saw the Orphans, not because she disliked them, still less because she had misgivings that following the precedent set by an older member of their family, whose movements were now somewhat circumscribed, one of the Orphans would behave in a startlingly unconventional manner. An incident of this sort had in fact taken place in the past which had resulted in authority discouraging the public appearance of this senior member of the family. Useful work therefore had been found for him at home, where the Orphans lived together in a cottage with a sister who shared their mental attitude and who did the cooking for them. Joanna knew of this incident, which had been described to her at some length by Mrs. Dadds, but her own imagination remained unexcited by the saga. Her curiosity was not stirred either. To Joanna indeed it seemed only a more highly coloured passage in the warp and woof of provincial life.

Joanna crossed the road because she had no money to speak of in her purse and, walking on the far side, the question of alms would not arise, because the Orphans had never explored the possibilities of stationing one of their number on each side of the street. Instead, the unoccupied pair stood at opposite ends of the organ and swept off the yachting-caps at everyone who passed. As a benefaction to the first of them did not absolve the donor from being pestered by the second, the pleasure of giving was considerably vitiated. At this time of day there was no traffic and the Orphan who was turning the handle did so lethargically and the notes emerged in an uncertain and strained way from the organ's lid. Like everyone else, the Orphans were affected by the prospective storm which seemed now as if it might burst at any moment.

Skirting the Orphans, Joanna crossed the road again, towards a door in the wall which led to the back of the house. She turned to see that Spot and Ranger were following her and watched them cross the soft macadam of the road, through the heat which quivered and shook above its surface. They reached the pavement, panting and asthmatic. *Les Cloches de Corneville* had become fainter as she came up the street, and when she put the key in the door she heard it change to *O sole mio*. She flicked Spot with the lead as he maundered over the threshold and, turning the key in the lock, she began to cross the lawn towards the house. There was not a breath of air and she felt the sun burning up the skin on the back of her neck. She approached the french windows of the drawing-room. These were shut. When she reached them Joanna did not go in at once but stood looking through them, standing a little at one side so that she could see into the room and avoid the reflection made by the sun on the glass.

Inside the room, beyond the french windows, her mother was lying on the sofa. Mrs. Brandon was not reading, although she was holding a magazine in front of her. She was holding it at too oblique an angle to make reading possible, but her lips were moving and she was smiling secretively to herself. The magazine was called *Everybody's Weekly*.

Joanna inspected her mother through the glass of the french windows. Mrs. Brandon was wearing a négligé of yellow material edged with fur, which stood out against the red and green roses of the chintz with which the sofa was covered, and the tartan rug and rather dirty counterpane that had also been spread over it, but which had by now almost slipped away from under her. The loose cover of the sofa was torn, so that a blue material could also be seen underneath it, and again, below this, some of the actual stuffing of the sofa itself, all this stratification suggesting the princess on her forty mattresses. Some books and magazines were within reach on an occasional table with a poker-work design on it that stood beside the sofa.

It was not impossible to see that Mrs. Brandon had been good-looking when younger. Her hair was still in places what she herself would have described as auburn and her features were good, although the powder which she had put on hastily and too thick obscured them and made her look like a favourite doll that has been worn to nothing by excessive use. It was said that she had been on the stage in her youth but she herself preferred to speak of any successes that she might have had behind the footlights as the result of an almost passionate interest in private theatricals. Anyway it had been a long time ago, before she was married, and she felt, rather justly, that it was nobody's business but her own.

When she had contemplated her mother sufficiently, Joanna pressed her hand against one of the french windows so that both of them flew open suddenly and banged against the walls of the room. She went in followed by the dogs. Without looking up, Mrs. Brandon said:

"I got tired of being here all by myself, darling, so I didn't wait for you and ordered tea earlier than usual."

A heavy perfume like the defensive cloud of a cuttlefish

hung round Mrs. Brandon. It was always the same scent. Jockey Club. The scent Mrs. Brandon had used since she had been a girl.

"Dr. Smith looked in this afternoon. He's not a very good doctor."

"What has he done now?"

"He doesn't seem to know what is wrong with me. Or, if he does, he won't tell me. He's not a doctor I feel I can rely on."

Joanna took off her hat and brushed away the hair from her forehead. She went to the big oval glass above the mantelpiece and looked at herself in it while she did this. Her forehead was too high and her hair mouse-coloured. She had a pale, very lovely skin and blue eyes. There was a certain aloofness about her appearance that distinguished her and made her the sort of girl with whom women might fall in love. Sitting down on the chair beside her mother, she poured out a cup of tea for herself.

"Pour me out another cup too, darling."

"I've just been to see about my shoes for the pageant."

"Have you, my pet?"

"I'm going to be one of the ladies-in-waiting to Charles II's queen, whoever she was."

"Do you know, Joanna, I always loved Charles II so much. He was always one of my heroes since ever I was a girl. I know he was a bad man but I simply couldn't help it. Perhaps it was a tiny bit because he was a bad man that I loved him so."

"And then I saw Major Fosdick in the town."

"Perhaps I even saw myself as Nell Gwyn. A little orange-girl. Pretty, witty Nell."

"Major Fosdick said that the Passengers have got a young man staying with them who has got a beard. At least Major

Fosdick says he has. Anyway I shall see when I go up for the rehearsal on Thursday."

"And how did dear Spot and dear Ranger enjoy their walk?"

"Spot was nearly run over by a boy on a bicycle. The Passengers are going to be here for the rest of the summer now, Major Fosdick says."

Ranger, who had been trying for some time to scramble on to the sofa, at last succeeded in his object and from this point of vantage found himself able to sniff at the plate of bread and butter. Mrs. Brandon went on with her reflections, still screened by *Everybody's Weekly.* Joanna drank two cups of tea and lit a cigarette. Then she went up to her bedroom. This was at the top of the house and from there it was possible to see the market square between the roofs. The Brandons' house was a red-brick, Queen Anne affair, and it had been very damp since Joanna's father had died, twenty-three years ago now. Her parents had married late in life and Joanna's father was said to have been one of the best-looking men in the Navy. He was just about due for promotion when one day, bathing, he had dived into the sea and on to a rock, killing himself instantaneously. He left no money worth mentioning, but he had bought the house and so, although it was absurdly large for two persons, Joanna and her mother continued to live in it. They kept one servant, Mrs. Dadds, who did the cooking.

Joanna went to her bookcase. She ran her fingers along the spines of the books, wondering whether there was anything that she could bear to read again. Outside, someone knocked on the door. It was Mrs. Dadds.

"Yes? What is it?"

"Mr. Jasper Fosdick to see you, Miss Joanna," Mrs. Dadds said.

"Tell him I'm out," said Joanna, through the door.

"I've told him you've just come in."

"Well, tell him I've gone out again and you made a mistake."

She heard Mrs. Dadds, still standing outside, breathing stertorously.

"Tell him anything you like," said Joanna, "that I've got a headache or I'm asleep or busy. Anything. I can't see him now."

Zouch and Mary arrived back at Passenger rather late for tea. This meal was taking place in a large room, decorated in the taste of a generation before and hung, like the hall, with anonymous and murky oil paintings. There had been one or two visitors, but they had gone and only the Passenger family now remained. When Zouch and Mary came in, Mr. Passenger was sitting a long way away from his wife and elder daughter, engrossed in reading a pamphlet. He barely looked up when Mary introduced Zouch to him.

"Did you decide to go to Goodwood in the end?" said Mrs. Passenger as she handed Zouch his tea.

They had met on several occasions when he had been to see Mary at their London house but Mrs. Passenger always confused him with another of Mary's young men, a young M.P. who had also for a short time worn a beard for political reasons.

"I didn't go," said Zouch, thinking it best to tell the truth.

He had begun suddenly to feel a little like a slum child and, never having been to a race-meeting in his life, he was not prepared to be cross-questioned about one, more especially as he was by no means certain that it was indeed racing that people went to Goodwood to watch. But he added:

"Did you?"

"I was going to stay with the Beckinghams. Vernon of course will never stay with anyone, and besides he hates racing. But in the end I said I wouldn't go. It's such a lovely house, isn't it?"

"Which house?"

"The Beckinghams'."

"I've never stayed there."

"But didn't you meet Mary there?"

"No," said Zouch.

He hoped that he would not have to divulge that he had met Mary at the house of a young married friend of hers who had since been divorced. He disapproved of divorces, knowing well that they were bad for business. Mrs. Passenger said:

"Oh, as a place I always think it is quite perfect. But too enormous and only three bathrooms. You have to see that you are given a bedroom near one of them. If you aren't, it spoils all the pleasure of going to Goodwood."

She sighed. She was a little wizened woman like a sea-bird and she came of a more distinguished family than her husband. As she stopped speaking Mr. Passenger looked up from his reading. The mention of the Beckinghams had jarred him into awareness of the presence of other persons in the room. He stared in front of him.

"Nonsense," he said.

"You have never stayed there, Vernon."

"I used to stay there when Tom Beckingham and I were at Eton."

"Then you can never have looked for the bathroom, Vernon."

Mrs. Passenger raised his eyebrows at his wife and then went on with his reading. He too, as Zouch had recognised at once, was an *Übermensch*. A pretty grim figure in fact. Indeed part of Zouch's uneasiness at that moment was due to an instantaneous fear that in Mr. Passenger he might have met his match.

People in the neighbourhood were accustomed to say that Vernon Passenger's manner was due to the disappointing life that he had lived. Hardly anything in his career had turned out as he had intended. As a young man he had become tired of London society and had gone out to the Boer war as a volunteer, but a few days after his arrival in South Africa he had nearly died of measles. When he came back to England and before he had fully recovered his health he began to edit the works of a seventeeth-century minor poet. But his convalescence had allowed him little time for research and the edition was found on publication to contain so many errors that he withdrew the whole of it at his own expense. This incident had given him a distaste for the life of the mind from which he had never wholly recovered and, as his father died about this time and he came into the property, he married at once and went to live in the country. There he occupied himself with the scientific growing of apples, crop after crop of which were destroyed every year by germs. Then the war came. Mr. Passenger had pro-German sympathies. Again he backed the wrong horse. It was no wonder that he was often morose. In winter he hunted, although the hunting in this part of the country was poor. He was Master of the local pack. In summer he prowled about quarrelling with his neighbours. He was an easygoing landlord, very popular with the cottagers, because he had once spoken over the wireless on an agricultural subject.

But all the time Vernon Passenger was gnawed inside with megalomania. He wanted to get away from all that he had been brought up to because it bored him and yet he felt that it was only by the accident of his position that he had any power at all. He used to brood over this,

longing to be something more, and yet knowing at the
same time that when he had come to live in the country he
had deliberately chosen to be what he was. What he wanted
to be he did not know. He knew only what he did not
want to be. By allowing this to work in his mind he
became every day more and more like what he wished
most to differ from.

Mrs. Passenger had, in fact, intended to marry another
man, better-looking but less intelligent than him, but she
came of a large family of daughters and the other man who
was eligible enough, became over-excited one night at a
dance and unexpectedly proposed to, and was accepted by,
one of her sisters. After that she decided to marry Vernon
Passenger, and, although after their marriage some of his
habits came as a surprise to her, she only sometimes regretted it because she was a woman with a serene tem-
perament and most of the time she had only a very vague
idea of what was going on round her. Mr. Passenger
himself sometimes liked his wife and sometimes disliked
her but from the earliest days of their honeymoon he had
made up his mind to brood about her as little as possible
and for many years now he had remained successfully
entrenched behind his own personality.

In appearance Mr. Passenger was not distinguished. His
lips and nose were too thick, and a casual observer might
have mistaken him, until they had encountered his con-
strained manner, for a dentist or professional man who rode
well to hounds. He had a high-pitched voice and when
spoken to was accustomed to look at the speaker for a few
seconds and then walk away without answering. And yet
Zouch knew that he was a dangerous man as soon as he set
eyes on him.

To bridge over the pause in the conversation, Zouch
said to Mrs. Passenger:

"What a lovely garden you have."

Before she could answer, her husband looked up again and, holding out to Zouch the pamphlet he had been reading, he said:

"Have you studied this yet?"

Zouch glanced at the title. It was called *The Powers and Duties of Local Authorities in Connection with Rural Amenities*. He shook his head. He could not imagine that a work with such a name would interest anyone to a great extent. He said:

"I haven't read it yet."

Mr. Passenger began to pick small pieces of fluff off his suit. He was, according to his usual custom, wearing out in the country clothes that were too old for London. His reddish face looked as if it had been scrubbed with emery-paper.

"Read it," he said. "It would interest you."

"I will."

Mr. Passenger said: "No one cares about the country now. People like you and me are the only ones left who mind whether or not the whole of England becomes an industrial suburb. We do what we can but it is too late."

"Yes," said Zouch, "I fear it is."

He was flattered at being included in this way by his host in the same category as himself, although the subject was one to which he had never given much thought in the past nor proposed to do so in the future, unless, as might well happen, it proved to be Mr. Passenger's only topic of conversation. He handed back the pamphlet. Mr. Passenger said:

"I suppose you are a Communist like all the rest of the young men now?"

No one was more convinced than Zouch that the existence of the fine arts depended on the survival of the capitalist system but considering that to express this verity would be to stress unnecessarily his status at Passenger Court he merely said:

"I don't know very much about politics."

"But no Communist ever considered that any bar to holding political opinions."

"I'm not a Communist anyway."

"Well, I think I am."

Mrs. Passenger said: "How absurd."

"All right," said Mr. Passenger. "Absurd."

"You're always saying things like that, Vernon."

"Mayn't I say what I like in my own house?"

Mr. Passenger shook his head once or twice, still plucking specks of grey from his trousers. Then he stood up and, after staring for a minute or two out of the window, he went out of the room, leaving the door open behind him. They could hear him in the hall tapping the barometer. Then they heard his footsteps become fainter as he went away down the passage. Betty said:

"Father seems rather off colour lately."

Mrs. Passenger said: "He's been interviewing old Fosdick about North Copse. And you know what that means."

"What a nuisance that old man is."

Mary said: "We met him while we were on our walk. He looked too extraordinary."

"I think old Fosdick will go off his head quite soon," Mrs. Passenger said. "His manner has been very odd lately."

Zouch, who was hemmed in by several little tables containing food, had begun to feel out of the conversation and so to make a digression he said to Mary:

"I shall hope to paint you, Mary, while I am staying here."

He was surprised at the effect this remark had. Mary

went quite pink with pleasure. It was evident that she was
delighted. She said:

"Oh, that will be fun. I've never had my portrait painted
before. Where would be the best place to do it?"

"Somewhere where the light is good and preferably where
the things can remain undisturbed."

"I'll go up to the old schoolroom and see if it is full of
rubbish. If it is, we will have it all cleared out and you can
do it there. That would be a splendid place."

She jumped up, looking remarkably pretty, Zouch
thought, and went out of the room. Betty lit a cigarette.
She said:

"Well, well, well. Are you going to paint all of us?"

Mrs. Passenger said: "Mr. Zouch will certainly not be
allowed to paint me whether he wants to or not. That is
quite definite. And now I am going to write some letters.
Don't scatter ash all over the carpet, dear. It makes such a
mess when you do that."

She wandered about the room for a few minutes as if she
were looking for something and then, giving up hope of
finding whatever she wanted, she went away. Zouch and
Betty were left alone together. Zouch said:

"Anyway, I hope I shall be allowed to do a portrait of
you one of these days even if I mayn't paint your mother?"

"Anything you like," said Betty. "If the old face is any
good to you. By the way, I think I've remembered where it
was that I saw you before. It was years ago at Zelli's. You
were with that little Creole that they used to call Hortense.
You were pointed out to me as the lucky man."

As Betty seemed to see nothing startling in this and as it
was possible that she was equally well informed about other
episodes in his past life, Zouch decided that once again it
was an occasion to tell the truth, and so he stroked his
beard and said:

"Quite likely. That would have been some years ago."

"About five years or even more."

"Did you know all the crowd who went about with her at that time?"

"Only a few," Betty said. "I knew rather a different lot then. Richer and more boring. But I knew some of them and I believe I once met Hortense. But how in the world did you come to be asked down here by Mary? You're more like one of my friends. I thought Mary only liked young men in the Foreign Office or the Brigade. She's always been terribly shocked by the people that I know."

"Has she?"

He was anxious to discover more about Betty's life in order to consolidate with this information his own position in regard to her. While he was doing this it would be as well to find out about Mary too. Betty said:

"Shocked? I should think she has. I always imagined that she was cut out for a thoroughly stuffy existence. But I see that there is hope for her yet."

"When did you decide that you wanted a change yourself?"

Betty said: "Well, I decided it pretty early on but I didn't do anything about it for some time. I only did something about it when I discovered that I had some money of my own. You can take it from me that we poor girls have a terribly hard time of it if we haven't any money. Fortunately a great-aunt left me and Mary a little so that if Mary ever wanted to cut loose she'd be able to do so as I did. But then she never will."

"Won't she?"

"Mary will marry some nice little younger son. She's not at all ambitious, you see. She just likes a quiet life."

"And what do you like?"

Betty, without extinguishing her cigarette, threw what

remained of it into the fireplace, where it lay sending up a wisp of smoke. She clasped her fat little hands together and said :

"Me? Well, I've liked a good many thing in my time. You should have seen my husband. The most wonderful profile you ever dreamt of. Rudolph Valentino simply wasn't a starter. Of course I didn't know how queer he was when I married him. Did you ever meet him? He was called Umberto. He was also called the *Duca di Civitacampomoreno*, but no one ever took that very seriously except himself."

"I think I was introduced to him once at the *Bœuf*."

"Yes, he liked the lads at the *Bœuf*. I used to like that sort of thing too in the old days and I had a fine time of it for a bit after I walked out on him. But you get tired of it. So I thought I'd come back and live in the country. It's better for the nerves. And besides I have such awful taste in men that I knew I should get into a real mess if I went on the way I was going. And then there was Bianca growing up."

"Who is Bianca?"

"My small daughter."

"What did your family think about it all?"

Betty lit another cigarette. She said :

"They've always been a bit vague about what exactly did happen after I was married, and anyway they knew damn well that I should be less nuisance here than anywhere else, so here I am. I just go about doing good, and falling for all the pansies in the neighbourhood."

"I see."

"It's not such a bad life."

Zouch did not answer. His feelings had been profoundly outraged. It was bad enough that he should find someone staying in the house who knew such details about himself

as his attachment to Hortense, but that this person should be
his host's daughter, and that she should combine this knowledge with talking the language of any little model of his
acquaintance, was genuinely distressing. He realised now
why Mary had mentioned her sister to him so seldom. He
became all at once aware of how much he himself disliked
people with Betty's attitude towards life. He was surprised
into silence and it was a relief to him that at this moment
his attention was diverted from Betty's display of bad taste
by the rattling of the door-handle and immediately after by
the entry into the room of a child, a little girl of about five
or six years old, with a snub nose and a peculiarly malicious
expression. There could be no doubt that this was Betty's
daughter. The child stood swinging backwards and forwards on the door-handle. Betty said:

"Hallo, poppet."

"Hallo," said the child, looking at Zouch.

"Come and say how do you do to Mr. Zouch."

The child moved slowly forward towards Zouch and, ex-
tending her hand, said:

"I've seen him already."

"You can't have done, sweetheart. He's only just arrived
here."

"I saw him in the morning-room this afternoon. He saw
me too but he didn't stop."

"Darling, I'm sure you didn't. What were you doing
there? You haven't seen Bianca yet, have you?"

Stealthily removing with his handkerchief some viscous
matter that had adhered to his fingers after Bianca's hand-
shake, Zouch said:

"No, I don't think we have met before."

He had no great objection to children and had often
found that to spend a few minutes playing with them was
an admirable method of convincing people that he had a

heart, if not of gold, at least of some almost equally precious substitute. Betty said:

"What were you doing in the morning-room, Bianca?"

"Reading the paper."

"What paper?"

"*The Times*."

At this moment Mary came into the room again. She was still flushed.

"Oh, hallo, Bianca," she said. "Have you been introduced to Mr. Zouch?"

"Yes."

"I had a look at the old schoolroom," Mary said. "There's every sort of thing in it at the moment but I've told Marshall to clear it up a bit. It's beautifully light."

Bianca said: "What are you going to do in the big schoolroom, Mary?"

"I'm going to have my picture painted."

"Can I too?"

"I daresay Mr. Zouch will paint yours too if you ask him nicely."

"Will you?"

"Yes," said Zouch, "I'd like to paint Bianca very much."

"Will it be funny?" Bianca said.

"You bet it will," said her mother.

Mary said: "Well, that is rude after he has been kind enough to say that he will paint your horrid child."

"Will he do it now?" said Bianca.

She took Zouch by the arm and began to swing up and down on it as she had done on the handle of the door.

TWO

Torquil Fosdick bicycled slowly along the High Street, planning great things. It was his second long vacation from Oxford, from which he had been sent down for a term for failing to pass an examination. He was at one of the smaller colleges, the members of which, although in their cups they sometimes ill-treated him, were secretly rather proud of his appearance and ways and the fact that he had found admittance to circles which those of them who could read knew of, but only from the diligent study of novels about Oxford. The secretary of the college hockey club, bemused one night with a couple of glasses of port stood him by his tutor, had entered Torquil's rooms by mistake for his own and had noticed there a distinct smell of incense. This had made him suspicious at once, and from that moment Torquil, who was himself only very dimly aware of the wonders of nature, achieved a reputation for profligacies which had rarely if ever crossed his mind. But when he was at home he burnt hardly any incense at all and occupied himself for the most part in country pursuits, which he enjoyed on account of his keen sense of social life. He was indeed at this moment bent on a mission to promote conviviality.

He met Joanna by the war memorial. She had been doing the day's shopping and had a basket on her arm. Torquil liked Joanna in a detached sort of way because she was the only person in the neighbourhood who had ever read any of the same books as himself and so he stopped and got off his bicycle and raised his hairy grey soft hat.

"Hallo, Torquil," said Joanna.

The weather was still hot and she disliked any business that had to do with housekeeping. Torquil smoothed back his hair and put his hat on again. Then he said in his grandest manner:

"Joanna, will you accept an invitation to my cocktail party at the Fox and Hounds?"

Joanna had never in her life been to a cocktail party although she had in fact drunk a cocktail before dinner at the house of some people who lived near, whose party she had been in for the hunt ball earlier in the year. The circumstance when considered in relation to the number of times that she had read about such entertainments made it clear to her that here was something not to be missed, although in Torquil's hands its form might well be of an unaccustomed order. She said:

"Of course I should love to, Torquil. When is it going to be?"

Torquil hunched his shoulders slightly and began to flap his disproportionately large hands.

"That's not decided yet," he said. "I'm on my way to the Fox and Hounds now to arrange all that with Captain McGurk."

"Who is going to be there?"

Torquil squirmed from the hips. He twisted his face into a mysterious expression and said:

"Well, I haven't decided that altogether yet, either."

"I suppose I oughtn't to have asked you."

"No, you oughtn't, really. You see, I don't exactly know yet who will come. The Passengers, for instance. I expect Betty will, but I'm not sure about Mary. And then they've got someone staying there whom I'd like to get. He's Arthur Zouch. Quite a well-known artist."

"Oh, is he staying there?" said Joanna.

The name was unfamiliar to her and she wondered whether there was anywhere where she could look him up before she met him, if she did succeed in meeting him. This was clearly the young man with the beard, whose arrival Major Fosdick had reported.

"And then," said Torquil, "I thought I might get the Orphans to play their organ for some of the time."

"What a good idea."

"Do you think they would be too noisy?"

"In the room?"

"If it was a nice day we might sit in the yard overlooking the canal."

"That sounds lovely."

They stood looking at each other. Torquil had given his information to the accompaniment of so great an output of energy that he was now exhausted and Joanna herself wished to get away and consider at her leisure how exciting or not the party was likely to be. Torquil draped one of his legs over his bicycle again. He smiled wanly and said:

"I'll let you know when I have decided more about it all."

"Thank you so much, Torquil."

"Don't mention it to anyone."

"Of course not."

He rode away over the cobbles with bent shoulders. Senile decay seemed already to have laid its hand on him while he was still in the grip of arrested development. Prematurely young, second childhood had come to him at a time when his contemporaries had hardly finished with their adolescence. Joanna went on with her shopping. Things were looking up. Later on in the morning she met the two Miss Brabys, the daughters of the vicar. She was annoyed to find that these plain but kind-hearted girls had also been invited to Torquil's party and spoke of it as if it were no secret at all. It was just like Torquil, she thought, to make a mystery of a thing like that. At the same time she was glad that he was giving the party.

The storm did not break until Sunday morning. At Passenger Court they were hanging about, waiting to start for church. It was Zouch's custom to follow the religious observances of his hosts in all his visits, except in the case of strictly orthodox Jewish households, and he was wearing a quieter tie than usual and one of his less arty shirts. He had risen early that morning, intending to walk round the garden before breakfast, but the rain had made this impossible and now he sat on the sofa reading one of the papers. Outside it thundered every few minutes. A steady downpour was soaking the lawn. Every time the noise of the thunder came nearer Mr. Passenger said:

"It's only a matter of time before it strikes the house. It's the curse. Three times it will be destroyed by fire. I remember that every time there is a storm."

Mrs. Passenger said: "Oh come, Vernon. You never mentioned the story to me until two years ago and soon after you told me about it I found something of the sort in a novel that Mary had got from the library. I believe you read about it there and got muddled."

Mr. Passenger assumed a pitying expression but he did not answer his wife. He was in a bad mood that morning. His relations with Zouch had not yet stabilised. Mr. Passenger took every possible advantage that accrued to him on account of his age, position, and the fact that he was host, while in return Zouch presumed on his own standing as guest, allowed himself considerable latitude of behaviour on account of his profession, and extracted the utmost from his status as Young Man. He did all this only when necessary as a retaliatory measure, but, as Mr. Passenger disliked *prima facie* all guests brought to the house by his daughters, Zouch found that in self-defence he was compelled to call up his reserves quite often. But, like Zouch, Mr. Passenger himself recognised the presence of another superman and he had therefore not yet risked a frontal attack. However, his wife had annoyed him by contradicting and after a few minutes he cleared his throat and said:

"You're an artist, aren't you?"

"Yes," said Zouch, who was always prepared for the worst and had in the past got it too often to be made nervous by bugaboos of this kind. Mr. Passenger thought for a moment. Then he said:

"What do you think about Sargent?"

"I suppose he has his niche."

Zouch did not see why he should come out in the open after so slight an acquaintance. A pronouncement on such a subject might be used as a stick to beat him with for the rest of his stay.

"His niche?"

"His niche."

Mr. Passenger did not answer. He laughed dryly to himself. He never spoke to Zouch again about painting and as Zouch himself was too experienced ever to raise such a topic he never discovered what were in fact Mr. Passenger's views on Sargent, which were of no great interest to him except in as much as they affected the length of his visit. To what extent this did actually depend on Mr. Passenger he had been unable at present to discover. As the subject of art was evidently at an end for the morning he picked up the paper again but it contained nothing that could be considered even remotely interesting to an adult in full possession of his faculties and so he put it down and looked across to the desk where Mary was writing letters. He wondered whether those firm, decided features of hers meant that she would always want her own way or whether, when it came to brass tacks, she would crumple up like a girl he knew who was a waitress in a café-bar in Soho and who had much the same profile. It was evident that Mary was built for endurance, and twenty years hence she would look scarcely less handsome than she did at that moment. She had, too, what Americans called poise. He was still thinking about her when Mary sealed the last envelope and, looking up, said to him:

"Of course you will be able to stay for the pageant, won't you? It will be quite soon. We don't know the exact date yet, but quite soon."

Zouch glanced politely in the direction of Mrs. Passenger, who was reading a bulb catalogue with the help of a lorgnette. He said:

"I hope I shall be able to. It is so kind of you to ask me. It depends how things turn out. I hope to hear for certain the day after to-morrow. Do you think you could keep the invitation open until then?"

This was untrue. As far as he could see he had nothing to do for the rest of his life, but it seemed to let everybody down more lightly if he put it like that. Mary herself was not taken in. She was sure that he could and would stay. But like Zouch she felt that this was a better way of putting it and she admired him for expressing himself in similar terms to those which she herself would have used in his place. Mr. Passenger said:

"Have I really given permission for this mummery to take place in the grounds?"

"Don't be absurd, Father. Of course you have."

"It can't happen. The lawn will be ruined."

Mrs. Passenger said: "It can't possibly be altered now. It is all arranged. You can always go away for the day if you think it will be a bore for you. You said yesterday you had some things to do in London. We shan't want the car so why not go to London in it?"

"Then I am to be turned out of my own house, am I?"

"Please, Vernon, don't say things like that."

"Why am I always being made a convenience of?"

"That sounds like the car," said Mrs. Passenger in a voice that dismissed the subject. "Are you ready for church, Mr. Zouch?"

"All except my hat."

"Where is Betty?" said Mr. Passenger, who had now lost interest in the question of the pageant.

"She hasn't got up yet," Mary said.

Mr. Passenger said: "I wish I could stay in bed all the morning without any responsibilities. Unfortunately for me I have an example to set. What an easy time all you young people have. I envy you."

"Why do you go, Vernon, if it's one of the days when you are not feeling well? Why not stay here and do the cross-word puzzle? After all, Mr. Braby can always read the lessons himself."

"No, no. I'll go. It's my duty, I suppose."

"But why?"

"I'll go. I'll go."

Mrs. Passenger sighed. It looked as if it were going to be one of her husband's bad mornings. It was in this vein that they set out for church. As they were getting into the car Zouch said:

"Are we going to the grey church I can see from my bedroom window?"

"No, no," said Mr. Passenger. "We have to use the church in the town. The local vicar is a very tiresome fellow. He used to argue with my father about doctrinal matters and my father, who was a very devout man, once struck him with his open hand. Since then we've had to go to the town church. That was nearly fifty years ago now, and there is no way of getting rid of him, so we just have to wait. He's remarkably hale and hearty for his age but he can't live for ever. It's inconvenient, but there it is."

The car rolled along through the rain at about twenty-three miles an hour, passing bevies of country girls in smart little hats and bright mackintoshes riding on bicycles. The clatter of the thunder was now becoming more distant. The storm would be over by the time they came out of church. No one spoke much because it was one of Mr. Passenger's difficult days, though Zouch made a few remarks to Mrs. Passenger with regard to the harvest. Mary seemed as if she was half-asleep. They reached the town and, passing the Fosdicks' house, went across the market-place and turned off towards the church. The car drew up just short of the Orphans, who, by the terms of the bequest to them of their organ, were restrained from Sunday performances and were indeed under an obligation when in good health (which all the Orphans enjoyed to a remarkable degree) to attend divine service. The Orphans took no notice of the car's horn but, unexpectedly, the brakes worked and none of them was injured, nor was the wing buckled by the contact.

The Passengers, followed by Zouch, went into the church, a Norman building with a tower, both the inside and outside of which had been energetically restored. On one side there was a memorial window in mauve, yellow, pink, and green to the memory of Mr. Passenger's grandfather who (because the Passengers had a Whig tradition) had been an under-secretary in one of Gladstone's governments and who had always said that he had refused a peerage. The Passenger pew was in the front of the church and was therefore inconveniently situated for watching the rest of the congregation, but Zouch had been put in first, next to the wall, and without actually looking round he could from here cast an eye over a considerable body of the worshippers.

The Fosdick family were within his orbit. They were on the other side of the aisle, huddled up at the far end of their pew. Major Fosdick was in a trance. He was leaning far back in his seat staring cadaverously in front of him as if he saw a vision, and the sun, bursting suddenly from behind clouds, streamed in through the memorial window and poured green and mauve reflections over his face, giving the features the semblance of premature decay. Torquil, next to him, was trying to draw on or to remove a pair of tight lavender gloves, while his mother, a wild-eyed woman wearing a hat like a beehive, was whispering a mass of information—it might have been her memoirs or an epic poem—into the ear of her elder son. But Jasper sat beside her with his mouth open, deaf to the flow of words. It was possible that he could not hear on account of the speed at which Mrs. Fosdick was proceeding. He was sitting screwed round in the pew at an uncomfortable angle trying to watch Joanna Brandon and he wore a very shiny blue serge suit. Zouch had a better look at them during the First Lesson. The lessons were read by Mr. Passenger in a low voice, emphasising all the prepositions, a method which caused what he read to be barely intelligible even to those who were listening or who were near enough to hear him.

It was towards the end of the Lesson that Zouch caught sight of Joanna. She was sitting by herself in a pew behind the Fosdicks and hitherto his view of her had been stymied by Torquil's immense head. The rays of coloured sunlight that gave Major Fosdick's flesh its deathly mottle were yellow where they fell on her, cutting off and separating her head and shoulders from the rest of her body and from the people round her. He was reminded of a primitive of one of the less remote female saints. The dust rose up round her through the streaks of light like incense in some elaborate effort of cinema photography. Zouch thought of the cathedral scene in *Faust* and smiled to himself. He wondered who she was. Joanna, who had had a good look at him some minutes before, continued to gaze towards her left, at a commemorative brass on the church wall. Later there was the Litany, often a concomitant of Zouch's church-going. He leaned forward dyspeptically, thinking that he would ask Mary to sit for her portrait that afternoon. The service proceeded.

"Here endeth the Second Lesson," said Mr. Passenger and, returning to the pew, sat down heavily. The vicar gave out a hymn. As they stood up Joanna had another look at Zouch. It was certainly true that he had a beard. This seemed to her rather a pity. At that moment Jasper Fosdick turned and caught her eye and she picked up a hymn-book and began to look for the place, which she had forgotten to do until then because she was occupied with her thoughts. Zouch shared a hymn-book with Mary, but neither of them joined in the singing.

The sky outside was dark blue now and the sun had disappeared again behind banks of cloud. The storm had passed on towards the west and in the church the light hung about in glowing, transparent volumes. The organist began to play an uneven voluntary and the choir clattered out. Zouch followed the Passengers down the aisle and out into the churchyard where the green of the grass had become all at once unusually bright and the water was sparkling on the yew hedge. The Fosdick family were loitering in front of the porch and Joanna was standing among them, talking to Mrs. Fosdick. When Major Fosdick saw Mr. Passenger he said :

"Rotten weather, Passenger."

"We wanted rain. The farmers needed it."

"The farmers never know what they want."

"It's been dry for too long," said Mr. Passenger.

He was going to escape to the car but before he could get away Mrs. Fosdick abandoned Joanna and began to talk to Mrs. Passenger about the pageant committee. Joanna, to prolong her connection with the group, asked Torquil who were the most interesting undergraduates up at Oxford and Major Fosdick said to Zouch:

"Have they roped you into the pageant yet? This is my boy Jasper. I didn't catch your name when we met the other day."

"Zouch," said Zouch and nodded at Jasper.

He wondered whether he would manage to get a word with Joanna, who was herself wondering how she could get herself introduced to him. Mr. Passenger stood on the outskirts of the group, scowling at everybody, undecided how to behave to show to the fullest advantage the disapproval he felt for his family and their acquaintances. Joanna said to Mary:

"You've only just come down here, haven't you?"

"I haven't been here very long. I was staying with various people for a bit after the rest of the family came down here from London. What has been happening?"

"Nothing. It never does."

"Oh, but I think it does," said Mary. "I always look forward to getting back here especially after two or three months in London. London always seems just the same. One long rush all the time. I like being in the country so much better."

"Do you like London then?" said Zouch to Joanna.

He thought he might have to wait a lifetime if he waited for Mary to introduce him of her own initiative to Joanna. To say this he broke off in the middle of something that

Jasper had begun to explain about the pageant, leaving Jasper's words in mid-air. Joanna said:

"I've only been there a very few times in my life but I think I'd like it better than living here."

She looked at Zouch with her large blue eyes. Mary, seeing that there was nothing for it, introduced them. Zouch examined Joanna at closer range. She was better even than he had thought across the church. Joanna said:

"Are you going to be here for the pageant?"

"Yes," said Zouch, forgetting that he had not yet officially announced this.

"Oh, I'm so glad you have decided to stay," Mary said. "We must get Mr. Petal to find a part for you."

Mr. Passenger, who was becoming tired of all this talking, and who had been standing first on one foot and then on the other, said:

"I think we ought to be going home now."

"Won't you come and take pot-luck with us?" Mrs. Fosdick said, but Mrs. Passenger said that they would not do that, and she and Mary and Zouch were herded back into the car by her husband, but not before Zouch, who believed that time should never be lost, had succeeded in saying to Joanna, out of Mary's hearing, that he hoped that they would meet again at the pageant.

"There's going to be a rehearsal on Thursday," Joanna said, in a voice that implied that young men meant nothing to her and that she knew far too many of them as it was.

The Passengers' car drove away.

Joanna was left standing among the Fosdick family.

"Anyway," said Major Fosdick, "you will come and take pot-luck with us, won't you, Joanna?"

"Do what?"

"Take pot-luck with us?"

Joanna said: "Yes. I'd love to."

She was thinking that Zouch's beard was really a great mistake. Jasper was so surprised at her readiness to share a meal with them that he said:

"Oh, I say, Joanna. Will you really?"

Sitting round the Fosdicks' dining-room table and eating roast beef and Yorkshire pudding, Joanna had time to collect her thoughts. Major Fosdick was in one of his excitable moods and he squeezed her arm when he offered her a second helping. His wife talked incessantly about local gossip. Mrs. Fosdick was a gaunt woman whose untidy grey hair looked as if it might come down at any moment and who was fond of telling people that she was half Irish. Her two sons were silent for most of the meal, Jasper never taking his eyes from Joanna's face except to look at what he was eating. Sometimes not even then. Major Fosdick said:

"He's a funny fellow, Vernon Passenger. A bit grumpy sometimes, as I expect you've noticed. Can't think what's the matter with him often when you speak to him."

"Yes. I think he is sometimes," said Joanna.

She liked Mr. Passenger. When she was sixteen she had even thought him very attractive and had wished she could have married him and, although a greater maturity had altered this view of him, she still preferred him to Major Fosdick. She said:

"I suppose he gets annoyed running the place. It must be an awful bother when people won't pay their rent and all that sort of thing."

"Nonsense, nonsense," said Major Fosdick. "Any trouble he has of that sort is all his own fault, you may be sure. In some ways he is much too easygoing. And then he's impossible in others. Look how tiresome he has always been about North Copse. I've got the place on a lease and there it is. After all, a few birds are bound to find their way there. He must realise that."

"Oh, but didn't he say that he did realise that?" said Mrs. Fosdick. "He said that when he came round the other day."

"Why should he go on fussing about it then?"

"Well, and perhaps it's happened again," said his wife, with one of her Irish smiles.

Her husband was not in an Irish mood. He was, on the contrary, rather snappy. He felt he had been slighted in the churchyard.

"You know he owns so much of the land round here. He likes his own way."

"I know he does. But why should he?"

"But you're not forgetting all the years and years that the Passengers have lived here and all."

"After all," said Major Fosdick, who was becoming angry at his wife's persistence. "After all, who are the Passengers anyway? Just because they happen to have made a few good business deals in land at the time of George III I don't see why I should kotow to them."

"George," said his wife, shocked and quite forgetting her Irishness, "I don't think you ought to say things like that."

"Well, why shouldn't I?" said the Major, who was working himself up into a rage. "Perhaps you can give me a good reason. Who are they?"

"Mrs. Passenger was a Blyborough."

"Well, and what if she was? What if she was?"

"Don't be so violent, George dear."

"As a matter of fact, I believe we're connected with the Blyboroughs ourselves if you go back far enough."

"Oh, are we? How very interesting. You never told me

that before," said Mrs. Fosdick, hoping to change the subject.

"Of course I never said so before. Do you think I have nothing better to do than spend my time boasting to my own wife about my pedigree? As it happens, I am not absolutely certain that we are. We may not be. All I say is that we might easily be. That's not the point. You seem to think that just because Mrs. Passenger happens to have been a Blyborough before her marriage that I should go down on my bended knee before her husband and ask his permission for everything I do and every bird I shoot. I shan't do anything of the sort, however much you may wish it. I can't think what makes you say things like that?"

Major Fosdick's lower jaw ground furiously. He looked quite hot. He glared round the table at all of them. Mrs. Fosdick said:

"Oh, George, and I never said anything of the sort."

"Anything of what sort?"

"All you've been saying."

"I shall tell old Passenger just what I think of him if there is any more nonsensical trouble of this kind."

Mrs. Fosdick did not say anything. She saw that her husband was being a bolshevik and that in his present mood it was hopeless to expect him to be amenable to reason. Jasper said:

"Who was the merchant with the beaver?"

"That young fellow?" said his father. "He's a queer-looking chap, isn't he?"

"He looks a very passionate man," said Torquil. "He's quite a well-known painter. I expect he has a very interesting life."

"How on earth can you tell that?" said his brother. "I could hardly see him for his beard. How can you tell he's passionate?"

Joanna said: "Well, he'll come in very useful for the pageant anyway. We want everyone we can get, don't we?"

After lunch they sat in the drawing-room for a short time, drinking coffee, and then Joanna, who had not enjoyed the meal much, said that she thought she ought to be going back to see how her mother was getting on. Jasper jumped up at once and said:

"I'll come up with you as far as the house, Joanna. I'm on my way to the golf course anyway and I'll just get my clubs and my bike and walk with you. Give me time to slip some other clothes on."

"All right. I'll wait here."

Later they walked along the road that led through the centre of the town, which the rain, falling on the dust of the weeks before, had made thick with mud. Jasper walked along in silence for some time and then he said:

"Oh, I say, Joanna."

"Yes, Jasper?"

Some specific idea had evidently separated itself from the main bulk of Jasper's brain and was trying to struggle to the surface. He swallowed.

"You haven't changed your mind at all, I suppose?"

"No, Jasper, I'm afraid I haven't."

"You don't mind my asking you?"

"No, of course not. But don't ask me every time you meet me, will you?"

Jasper looked astonished. Agonised.

"Why not?" he said.

"Well, I mean it will become rather a bore, won't it?"

"To you?"

"Yes. And to you?"

"Oh."

They walked on for a while without speaking until they

reached the gate of the red-brick house. Jasper leaned on his bicycle. There was a pause. Joanna said:

"Well, good-bye."

Jasper waited, resting his foot on the pedal of his bicycle, breathing heavily. He seemed unwilling to go on. At last he said:

"I suppose you won't come and have a round now? You could play with my clubs. The bus is due at any moment and I could meet you at the golf-house."

"No, thanks."

"Sure?"

"Yes."

He moved off on his bicycle, waving but not turning round to look at her. Joanna slammed the gate. She went into the house. Her mother was as usual lying on the sofa. Mrs. Brandon was re-reading her favourite book, *The Story of San Michele*.

"Hallo, Mother," Joanna said. "I went back to lunch with the Fosdicks after church."

"Did you, darling?"

"It wasn't very amusing."

"Wasn't it, my pet?"

"It was very boring."

Mrs. Brandon made a little singing noise to herself, a brief arpeggio, to show that she was still listening. Joanna sat down. She said:

"Is that a good book?"

"It's a beautiful book, darling. A very beautiful book. It's a book that takes your old mother out of herself."

"Does it?"

"Why aren't all books that people write beautiful? Why don't writers only write about the beautiful things in life? You know, Joanna, there is so much beauty all round us."

"What has happened to the dogs? Why aren't they here?"

"Poor Spot has been sick."

"Again?"

"It was the mutton. I told Dadds not to give him the mutton. It was too stringy."

"I'll take him to the vet on Monday."

"Poor Spot must go see doctor. Give him nasty physic. Hand mother a cigarette, darling."

"I saw the young man staying with the Passengers. He has got a beard. It looks funny. But he seems rather nice."

"When I first met your father, Joanna, he wore a beard. I thought he was the most wonderful man I had ever seen. And he *was* the most wonderful man, Joanna. So tall and strong and sunburned. He looked like a Greek god. I remember once saying that to Vernon Passenger and him saying, 'And he used to behave like one too.' Wasn't that a tribute? From someone as critical as Vernon Passenger, too. Did I ever tell you how I first met your father, Joanna?"

"Yes, Mother, you've often told me."

"Are you quite sure?" said Mrs. Brandon. "It was one lovely day towards the end of June, what years and years ago it seems . . ."

Up in the old schoolroom at Passenger, Zouch began his portrait of Mary. It was a big, bare room at the top of the house, overlooking the park. The wallpaper, faded and in places blistered, was covered with a violent floral design and there was a broad frieze running round the top of the room. Now that the boxes had been cleared away the room seemed even larger because there were only a few pieces of battered furniture in it. Zouch arranged Mary on a Victorian red chair, in front of a screen covered with Pears soap advertisements of forty years earlier, cut out and varnished. Mary, who had never before had her portrait painted, was still excited and she continually asked Zouch if it would be like her and how long it would take to do. Zouch was enjoying himself. Here he was in a house where the food was good and his bed comfortable. He had a room to work in and he liked Mary. Things could hardly be better.

"A little more to the left," he said. "Look up a little."

Mary said: "But this is silly. It's like being at the photographer's."

Zouch laughed and scraped away at his palette. There were a number of things he wanted to make enquiries about and he decided that this might be a favourable moment to begin them. He said:

"Who was the girl we spoke to when we came out of the church? She was talking to the Fosdicks when we came through the porch. Do you remember?"

"She's called Joanna Brandon."

"What's she like?"

"She's not bad."

"She seemed rather nice."

"She's not very nice really. At least I don't like her very much. They live in the town. Her mother is rather an awful old creature. Joanna isn't bad really. She's rather—rather pretentious or whatever you call it. She tries to be a highbrow."

"Well, so do I. Not a very successful one perhaps. But still I try."

Mary laughed a lot. That sort of joke amused her because she was quite unused to people who said things like that. Zouch said:

"Now you have moved to quite a different position. But aren't you a highbrow too?"

"Me? No. Of course I'm not."

"No, perhaps you're not. That is why you are so nice."

"You are polite. Do you always say nice things like that when you paint people?"

"Always. I've got all sorts of other things rather like that which I'm going to say to you later on."

Mary laughed again. She was sure now that her instincts had been right when she had asked him to come and stay at Passenger. He was certainly unlike any of the other young men whom she knew. It was refreshing to meet someone who was so different. And then, thinking again of what he had been saying earlier, she said:

"Do you think Joanna Brandon pretty?"

"Who is Joanna Brandon?"

"I've just told you. The girl you were asking about. The girl we met after church."

"Oh yes, of course. You were saying that that was her name. Pretty? Well, I hardly noticed. I only spoke to her for a second."

"Some people think she is."

"Do they?"

Mary became quiet suddenly and did not speak for nearly two minutes. Zouch decided that if he did not bother her she would talk about Joanna of her own accord and he would find out anything there was to know. After a time Mary said:

"Torquil Fosdick is a funny boy, isn't he?"

"He certainly is."

"I should think he was—well, at least I mean, you know —at least I should think anyone would think so, wouldn't you?"

"Oh yes, I should think so. If they took the trouble to think about him, I mean."

"He is at Oxford, you know. He's just been sent down."

"Oh, has he?"

"Only for a term."

"Really?"

Zouch regarded both the universities as effete, but he kept this opinion to himself, as he found that persons who had been educated at them often disagreed with, and were irritated by, this conviction when he expressed it aloud. Not knowing what Mary's views might be he thought it better to change the subject and so he said:

"Tell me more about the pageant."

"It's quite a small one. Just scenes from the life of Charles II. He once visited the town, you know."

"Did he? Who is acting Charles?"

"Captain Hudgins-Coot. He's the hunt-secretary. They wanted father to do it but he wouldn't take part in it at all. I'm doing Lady Castlemaine. Betty is Nell Gwyn. Mr. Petal is organising it all and we must get him to find a part for you."

"What are the Fosdicks doing?"

"Major Fosdick is going to be General Monk. The two boys are courtiers. Rochester and somebody, I think. Doing Lady Castlemaine will be rather fun. I'm looking forward to it."

"Who was Lady Castlemaine?" Zouch said.

He did not know much history, though he remembered the essential facts about Nell Gwyn. He hoped he was not going to be let in for a lot of acting. Dressing up was the furthest he was prepared to go. Mary said:

"She was one of Charles's mistresses, you know."

She felt that she had brought the word out rather well. Zouch thought she had too. She said it in a way that showed that she was a broad-minded girl but at the same time was not at all indifferent, like her sister Betty, to wider moral issues. She said:

"I don't expect she had much of a time, poor thing, because he seems to have had a good many of them."

Zouch said: "Yes. I expect he did," and laughed.

But he felt that enough had been said for that afternoon about the seamy side of life.

"Can you sit a little more round this way?" he said. "Yes, like that. Excellent."

He wondered what part had been cast in the pageant for Joanna.

THREE

Betty Passenger and Torquil Fosdick walked together through the dust and up the hill leading out of the town towards the London road. Betty was carrying a tennis racquet, which she had picked up at a shop in the town where they had been mending one of its strings. She herself hardly ever played tennis and it was Mary's racquet which she had agreed to go into the town to collect for her, as Mary had something else that she wanted to do on that afternoon. Mary often used Betty for odd jobs of this kind, all of which Betty seemed prepared for. Passing the Fosdicks' house, she had looked in to see if Torquil was at home and, on finding him there, had suggested that he should walk some of the way home with her. When she walked Betty took long masculine strides and Torquil had to trot along quickly to keep up with her.

"Olives," she was saying. "You must not forget olives. They make all the difference to a party of that sort. And cheese straws."

Torquil said: "And then the Orphans. What about them? Do you think they will prefer cocktails or beer? I shall have to provide something for them. Perhaps beer would be better."

"And don't forget some cigarettes."

"Do you think Mary will come?"

"My dear Torquil, of course she will. I'll make her."

"Can you really?"

"Of course I can."

"And Mr. Zouch?"

"Yes, he'll come all right too. We'll all come. It's going to be a great party, Torquil."

"What is Mr. Zouch like?" Torquil said.

He hurried along, peering up at Betty with his little rat eyes.

"Shall I tell you?"

"Do tell me, Betty."

"He's lousy," Betty said. "But don't go and say I said so."

"My dear Betty, you know I should not dream of repeating such a thing. You can rely on me to be discreet."

"Oh, you're so sweet. I could bite you."

Torquil laughed a trifle nervously. He liked Betty. He enjoyed the fact that she was a duchess, even though it might be only a Neapolitan one. But sometimes he had no idea what she was talking about and she alarmed him more than a little. They went on up the hill. Torquil said:

"But what is it you don't like about Mr. Zouch?"

He knew Zouch's name from reading art-criticisms and he was anxious not to miss a lion of this kind.

"Is he very *difficile*?" he said.

"No, he's a damn sight too *facile*," Betty said. "He's an ambitious little brute whom Mary has taken a great fancy to for some reason. She'd have a fit if she knew some of the things about him that I do."

"Really *bad* things?" asked Torquil hopefully.

"Oh, no. Just dreary things."

"What sort of things?"

Betty said: "I can't possibly tell you now. It would take all the afternoon. He's just awful and there it is."

Torquil was disappointed. He said:

"Still, you'll bring him to my party, won't you?"

"Don't you worry. He'll come without you asking him, if he hears that there is a party anywhere near."

"Oh, Betty, I feel sure that he would not. No one would go to a party unasked. Even at Oxford there are people who wouldn't do that."

"I just love to hear you talk. It's wonderful. Like a tonic."

Torquil was embarrassed.

"Am I being a bore, Betty?" he said.

"A bore? You know, Torquil, I don't know what I should do without you here. I need looking after and nobody ever takes any notice of me except you."

"Oh, but, Betty, you can't say that. You've lived. You've had adventures. Known famous people. I'm still at Oxford."

"That doesn't matter," Betty said. "It doesn't depend on what you've done. Look at Mary. She's never had any experience, but she knows how to look after herself far better than I do. Look at Jasper. He's had plenty of experience and look what he is, even though he is your brother, my pet."

Torquil felt that he was getting into deep water. He said:

"Anyway, I want to live too."

"You shall," said Betty. "One of these days I'll take you out and show you people and then you'll be able to judge for yourself. You can choose what you like from the whole cockeyed world."

This sort of talk made Torquil quite breathless.

The rehearsal of the pageant which took place some days later was not much to Zouch's liking, but he saw that in the near future he would have to put up with a good deal of that sort of thing and so he did what seemed to be required by politeness and then sneaked away to smoke a cigarette in the morning-room. A deserted part of the garden would have been more pleasant but he did not know when the focus of the pageant might suddenly remove to any secluded spot chosen by him. He left Mary and Betty listening to a disquisition on deportment from the lips of Mr. Petal, the master of the ceremonies. Joanna was present but he had not yet had an opportunity to approach her. When he reached the morning-room he found to his annoyance that Jasper Fosdick was already sitting there on the sofa. Jasper said:

"Hallo. So you've slipped away too, have you?"

Thinking it unnecessary to admit verbally that such was the case, Zouch replied with a special sort of leer and, walking across the room, took a cigarette from the box. Here away from the crowd he was beginning to recover his superman technique which had been threatened momentarily by the number and unfamiliarity of those taking part in the rehearsal. He sat down in one of the arm-chairs. Jasper said:

"A chap doesn't want to do that sort of thing all day."

"Hardly."

"After a bit you want a sit-down."

"Certainly you do."

"You're staying here, aren't you?"

"Yes."

"Have you known the Passengers long?"

"Yes."

"Know this part of the country well?"

"No," said Zouch, "I don't."

He had begun to feel irritable. This person, by all appearances a moron, seemed to be preparing to put him through the third degree. To turn the tables, he said:

"Do you live here?"

"Just outside the town. In a house called Widemeadows.

The one with chains in front of it. And I say, old man, is that a Toc H tie you're wearing?"

Zouch was not going to stand much more of this sort of thing. He said: "Do you enjoy living in the country?"

"Well," said Jasper, screwing up his face, "it's not so bad. Do you play golf?"

"No."

"There's golf. And then I go zooming round in the family Ford. She's not a bad old bus when you know the trick of cranking her up."

"She isn't, isn't she?" said Zouch. "And what else do you do?"

A puzzled look came over Jasper's face. He wore no suspenders and he began thoughtfully to pull up the thick woollen socks that hung in corrugations about his crêpe-rubber-soled shoes.

"Oh, there's plenty to do," he said, "though I suppose I stay put most of the time. You see I don't seem to be much good at jobs. I've had a good many of them in my time, though. You'd be surprised if I told you about all the jobs I've been in, off and on. But I'm like Betty Passenger. I've made a mess of my life."

"How do you mean?"

"Oh, I don't know. You've heard all about her of course?"

"She married someone rather awful, didn't she?"

"An Italian. She's a duchess. Did you know that?"

"Yes."

"Her husband was called the Duke of Something-Moreno. She met him at a night-club in London and insisted on getting married. Moreno thought that all English ladies had lots of money and when he found that she had hardly any at all he deserted her in Paris. Or she left him. I can't remember. Anyway no one knows exactly what she did for a year or two. But after a time she came back home and settled here."

"But what has that got to do with you?" said Zouch. "Did you make an unfortunate marriage too?"

Jasper said: "Oh no. Nothing like that. But I mean both Betty and I haven't got much to do here, if you know what I mean. We just sit around. We don't seem to belong somehow."

"But Betty is quite happy, isn't she? With her daughter and so on?"

"Oh yes. She seems all right really. I don't think she is in love or anything awful like that."

"You speak as if you yourself were suffering from something of the sort."

Jasper lay back on the sofa and stretched his legs in front of him. He was wearing a pair of flannel trousers that had seen better days. Or, if not better, at least cleaner ones. He stared fixedly at the ceiling and pulled at his rank moustache hairs. He said:

"You've said it. That's what's wrong with me. I'm in love."

Zouch thought to himself that this was not by any means the only thing that was wrong with Jasper. He wondered who was the object of this clod's affections. It occurred to him that it might be Mary Passenger. His curiosity was aroused and he said:

"Is she here to-day?"

"Is she? I should say she is."

"Taking part in the pageant?"

"Rather."

In moments of excitement Jasper's speech faltered between ill-imbibed patter culled from the talkies and the argot of wartime musical-comedy, imperfectly remembered. Their combination was impressively individual so that by his presentation of these modes of speech he managed to exclude from each any forcefulness of expression that might be thought to have been inherent in them.

"Fair or dark?" Zouch said.

A little jocularity might get it out of him. Zouch was quite curious to know which of the girls taking part in the pageant—not a very interesting crowd on the whole—had captivated Jasper.

"She's in between," Jasper said. "Neatest little figure you ever saw. Of course I know I'm not half good enough for her and all that, but all the same a chap can't help falling in love, can he?"

"No," said Zouch, "I suppose he can't."

"The trouble is she's clever. She's always reading books."

"Is she?" said Zouch, thinking that the delineation sounded familiar.

He felt sure that there could not be many girls in the neighbourhood to whom this description might be said to apply. If his suspicions proved to be correct, here was a funny situation. He said :

"I daresay her home life isn't any too cheerful either?"

"You're quite right. It's not. But how the dickens did you guess?"

"Is it the girl who stood on the left of the steps when the king and queen came down them?"

Jasper's lower jaw, always a subordinate feature in his face, went limp. He ruffled up his hair, already untidy enough, with one hand and plunged the other more deeply into his pocket. He said :

"Now how the deuce could you have guessed that it was Joanna? Have you met her?"

"Joanna? Joanna? What is her surname? It was only that I noticed you glance several times in that direction when she was coming down the steps."

"She's called Joanna Brandon. That's her. You've got it in one."

"Joanna Brandon? Oh yes, I believe we were introduced on Sunday after church. But really I had no idea that it was her you meant. It just struck me as a possibility."

"No. That's her. You've hit the nail on the head. You see she wants to get away from here. She's tired of living here. I don't blame her. And marrying me would mean living here. I know that's why she won't do it. That must be it, mustn't it?"

"Oh, obviously," said Zouch. "But why does she want to get away from here so much?"

Jasper raised his eyebrows in a series of grimaces, each less inviting than the one that had preceded it. Towards the close of these contortions his face began more and more to resemble his father's. He continued to scratch his head.

"It's her ma," he said.

"Her ma?"

"Her father died years ago. He was a sailor. He and Mrs. Brandon used to fight like one o'clock. She was an actress at one time, you know. Joanna's father used to be great friends with old Passenger. That was why he came to live here, but Mrs. B. didn't like the Passengers because she thought they high-hatted her. Then, when her husband died, she said she would be like Queen Victoria and never be seen in public again. It was really an excuse because she hated taking exercise. Nobody minded about it but it's tough luck on Joanna. It's made her a bit strange you know. She sits about reading a book all day long. Of course I daresay reading is in the blood and she does it naturally like her mother does. Still, you'd think she'd like to come and have nine holes with me once in a while, wouldn't you?"

"Yes," said Zouch, "I should think so. If her life is really as dull as you prepare me to believe."

"Not a bit of it," said Jasper. "She always makes some excuse or other. No clubs or a headache or something of the sort. I have no patience with her. Do you know that once or twice I've almost thought that she didn't want my company?"

"Women are queer."

"You're quite right. They're—I don't know—somehow— different from men in a way, don't you think?"

"Aaah."

"That's it. You don't know altogether where you are with them. They're funny, somehow."

"Is Miss Brandon like that often?"

"Joanna? Good Lord, no. She's a topping girl really. A genuine good sort. But, you know, she gets a bit snappy sometimes, just as we all do. I don't take any notice. I stay away for a day or two and then drop in about tea-time to see if she is in. Trouble is she's out sometimes and I have to sit and talk to the old girl."

"But what is wrong with Mrs. Brandon?"

"Oh, I suppose there isn't anything wrong with her really. She's just a bit odd. Talks to you as if you weren't there. Gives me the creeps properly. And, I say, by the same token, don't get huffy, but why do you wear a beard?"

"Because I like the feel of it," said Zouch.

He had often been asked the question before and was quite prepared for it. He sometimes even welcomed it as a good opportunity for describing himself to people from his own point of view. But now he had a growing perceptivity that his byssine days were drawing to a close and that with a newly acquired social consciousness he would soon do better with bare cheeks. He could sense that change was in the air. A change for the better. But still while he wore a beard it was his duty to stick up for it. Jasper said:

"No offence and all that, but I mean it makes a chap wonder when he sees a face-fungus like that on a fellow. I mean it quite put me off at first. I thought you'd be like goodness knows what to talk to. Besides it must be awfully uncomfortable, isn't it?"

"On the contrary."

"Well, I should never have thought it. It makes you look like an artist or something."

"I am an artist."

"Good Lord, are you?"

"And why not?"

"Oh, I don't know. Seems funny somehow. Are you painting old Passenger's picture or something?"

"He has not asked me to yet," said Zouch, who was beginning to feel uncommonly tired of Jasper's company, "but I daresay I may do so later on during my stay."

He rose from his chair and again walked across to the cigarette-box, from which he filled his case. Looking through the window he saw that the sky had clouded over. As he felt that he had now had enough of Jasper, he put the cigarette-case back into his pocket and went leisurely from the room. Behind him he heard Jasper say:

"You aren't in a huff, are you?"

Zouch went into the hall, towards the door that led to the garden, which might have been reached more easily by the french windows of the morning-room. He did this to cover his tracks from Jasper in the event of possible pursuit. When he came to the threshold of the door he found that clouds were gathering over the house and, stepping out on to the path, he looked up. A heavy drop of rain fell on his face. He stood for a moment undecided what to do, watching the rehearsal which had now moved to the corner of the lake and stood grouped round Mr. Petal, who, with his fine crop of white hair falling now and then over his eyes, was walking mincingly up and down, exhibiting to the rest of them the demeanour of some Caroline celebrity. The potential mummers stood around him, rather grimly, as if they were taking part in a political demonstration. At moments they would start and look upward, holding out the palms of their hands to assure themselves that it was indeed rain that they felt. And then, all at once Mr. Petal paused with startling suddenness, one arm raised in the air. He too gazed into the sky for a few seconds, and then with a sweeping gesture conveying in its scope, rage, despair, thwarted ambition, contempt, defiance, disbelief in the goodness of human nature, and a stumbling hope in some pantheistic creed, he indicated the house with his unnaturally long forefinger. The rehearsal began to move in a mob across the lawn towards the door where Zouch was standing. The rain was coming down faster now and the people who had at first walked slowly, talking to each other, now began to run. They were headed by the two Miss Brabys, daughters of the vicar. Zouch stepped inside to avoid being seen. Indoors these people would be worse even than in the garden. A decision must be made. He therefore walked away through passages into a nondescript wing containing the billiard-room and kitchen which enclosed one side of a yard in front of the stables. Here he was unlikely to be disturbed. Marshall, the butler, passing in his shirt-sleeves, eyed him balefully, but said nothing more than:

"Wet, sir."

"I'm afraid so."

"Been hanging about all the week."

"It has."

Marshall disappeared into his pantry, gently slamming

the door behind him, and inside Zouch could hear him singing hoarsely to himself, "*I'm just a girl that men forget—just a toy to enjoy for a while*." Zouch lounged in the doorway looking on to the yard, watching the rain, unable to go out, unwilling to return to the habitable part of the house, from which he could already hear the sound of many voices. To make matters worse he recognised in himself the symptoms of a growing feeling of social misgiving. He debated retiring to his bedroom until the reheasal died down. He pulled at his beard.

While he was thinking, he saw that someone was running across the yard towards the doorway in which he stood. It was a girl, and she was holding a newspaper over her head to keep off the rain, hiding her face in this way so that it was only when she was quite close that he realised that she was Joanna Brandon. She hurried on towards the door and because she did not see that he was standing on the threshold she would have run into him if he had not stepped aside. Zouch saw that this was his chance. The chance that was usually offered to him at least once in these matters. As usual, too, it had come at a time when he was not feeling at the top of his form. He said:

"Where have you been? The others came in as soon as the rain started."

She crushed the newspaper up into a ball suddenly and held it in front of her, staring at him with her large eyes. He saw again that she was slim and held herself well. They were still standing absurdly close to each other but neither of them moved. Joanna said:

"One of the halberds got left behind and I went to put it away."

She looked at him without smiling. Zouch was surprised to find himself all at once quite out of breath with excitement. He said:

"Oh?"

"I suppose everyone has come into the house now?"

"Yes."

There was a pause. Joanna cleared her throat a little. Zouch wondered whether it would be better to talk himself or to make her talk. He felt that he was not so much master of himself as he was accustomed to be on such occasions and he attributed this deficiency to unfamiliar surroundings and problems. Joanna said:

"We met on Sunday, didn't we? After church."

She moved away a little and looked on the ground. Zouch decided to take the offensive. After all, old-fashioned methods were often the best ones. They had been hallowed by centuries of success. He said:

"Has anyone ever told you what pretty eyes you've got?"

"Has anyone ever said that to me, did you say?"

"Yes."

Joanna said: "As a matter of fact someone is always telling me that. He says it whenever he sees me. But that's as rarely as I can manage because he is rather a bore."

"Do you think I am likely to be a bore too, now that I have said it?"

"I don't know at all."

"How discouraging."

She laughed.

"No," she said. "I don't think so. In fact I'm sure you're not. But why do you wear a beard?"

Zouch said: "That is the second time in five minutes that I have been asked that question. I'll tell you. It's because I think it suits me."

"Do you?"

"Don't you?"

"No."

Zouch said: "I expect that is only because you are not

used to beards. They can look very distinguished really. And, by the way, it isn't because I've got a weak chin. I happen to have a very good chin."

He was aware that matters were moving too fast. His technique had got out of control. Unless there was a slow-up he might make a mess of things. In a few seconds he saw that his misgivings were justified. She could not think of anything to say in answer to his last remark and, what was worse, she began to hum and to play about with the string of heavy beads that hung round her neck. It was possible that the spark had been struck too early. Although he was naturally insensitive to the personal feelings of other people, Zouch was by instinct unusually responsive to the implications of a situation and he was anxious that any magnetism there might be should not be dissipated uselessly at this first encounter. He said:

"But don't let's talk about my beard. Come and tell me all about the people in the pageant. You see I don't know any of them. And besides, this passage is rather uncomfortable. Shall we find somewhere to sit in the hall?"

"Yes, if you like."

"Come along then."

He remembered that there was an alcove under the sweep of the stairs which had the advantage of a certain privacy without any of the opprobrium that might attach, should anyone happen to discover them, to some more remote part of the house. It would be unwelcome certainly for Mary to find them together having a tête-à-tête after so slight an acquaintance, but that was the worst that could happen. He noticed that Joanna was a little flushed but she was so pale that this brought her complexion to a tone not much deeper than Mary's normal pink and white. Zouch began to move off sideways down the passage. Joanna followed him. Like Zouch she knew that somehow

an issue had been forced and this made her awkward,
because having none of his experience and being not at all
opposed to the course that he seemed to intend that matters
should take, she thought that perhaps in some way un-
known to herself she had already ruined everything. She
walked down the passage beside him. Marshall opened a
chink of the pantry door as they passed but shut it again
when he saw them and went on with his singing and
they reached the hall without encountering anyone else. A
party of people who had been taking part in the rehearsal
were on the steps of the house and preparing to get into
a car and drive home, but these were too engrossed in
grumbling about the rain to notice anyone else, and skirting
the stairs, Zouch and Joanna sat down on an uncouth piece
of furniture, Tudor and intensely uncomfortable, which
stood at the back of the alcove. Zouch had decided that the
only thing to do was to start again at the beginning. He
said :

"You live near here, don't you?"

"Yes. In the town."

"Is it fun?"

"Fun. Goodness, it's the most awful thing in the world.
It was more fun when I was at school."

"But why? There seem to be all sorts of excitements.
This pageant, for instance?"

"Of course if you think this sort of thing is fun. Anyway
where were you most of the time? I only saw you right
at the beginning of the afternoon."

Agreeably surprised to find that she had noticed his absence from the later stages of the rehearsal, Zouch said :

"Well, what sort of a life would you like to lead
instead?"

"I should like to be in London. To live by myself and
work."

"But how do you know what that would be like?"

"I've read about it of course."

"Oh, you've read about it, have you?"

Zouch himself did not care for reading, except a few favourite books like *The Way of all Flesh* and *Moby Dick* and *The Four Just Men*, all of which he would read over and over again, and reading was a habit he discouraged in the women with whom he was associated. He had noticed that it was inclined to make them over-critical. Now he remembered Jasper's warning about Joanna's taste for books. He said:

"Working in London would not be at all like the sort of thing that you have read about in novels."

"Of course it wouldn't. I never said it would."

"But you seem to think that living in London must necessarily be great fun."

"I don't in the least."

It seemed possible that they were heading for another impasse. Zouch saw that she was not going to be an easy girl to manage and he surprised himself by the trouble he was taking to establish a satisfactory emotional contact with her. To change the subject he said:

"I know. I'm sure you don't. But I myself feel so glad to have got away from London for a bit that I could not imagine anyone wanting to be there. But don't let's quarrel about that. Tell me more about yourself. How did you come over this afternoon?"

"In the Fosdicks' car."

"The famous Ford?"

"How do you know that they have a Ford? Or that it is famous? You don't live here. Did Mary Passenger tell you about it?"

"I've just been having a chat with Jasper."

"Oh, I see."

He saw her glance at his face and knew she was wondering whether Jasper had said anything to him about herself. Then she said:

"How do you like Jasper?"

"I don't know him very well yet."

"But from what you have seen of him?"

Before he could decide what was the best verdict to give on Jasper, taking into consideration that clearly she thought him a bore but at the same time she might reasonably be supposed to have some friendly feeling towards someone who was so much attached to her, Zouch was interrupted in his speculations by a voice saying:

"So there you are, my dear. I have been looking for you everywhere. We are on our way back now."

He looked up and saw Torquil Fosdick, who stood watching them with his huge head swaying from side to side. He appeared to be in labour with some formidably witty remark which never managed to achieve parturition. In the end he smiled again weakly and said:

"The car is quite ready."

Joanna slid off the thing they were sitting on and stood up, rubbing herself for a few seconds at the relief from its wooden discomfort. As Zouch and Torquil did not speak,

"You both know each other, don't you?"

Torquil muttered something which Zouch hardly took the trouble to answer. He felt that he had already got on far too intimate terms with Jasper and did not want to embarrass himself with Torquil's acquaintance also. Somewhere near they heard Betty's voice shouting:

"Torquil! Torquil!"

"Here I am."

"Where?"

"Here. Under the stairs."

Betty came round the corner and into the alcove.

"Hallo, handsome, so there you are," she said to Torquil. "You left your lovely gloves in the drawing-room. You'll be forgetting them if you aren't careful."

She handed Torquil the gloves and looked round at the others.

"Why are we all sitting here?" she said.

Torquil said: "I came to say that the car was ready now and to ask Joanna if she wanted a lift back."

"Don't go yet. There's no hurry, is there?"

"Jasper has got the engine going and we don't want to turn it off in case it won't start again."

"Leave it running then and stay for a bit."

"We've only just got enough petrol in the tank to get back. We must go."

"I'm ready," said Joanna. She turned to Zouch.

"I hope we shall meet again," she said.

When she said that, Zouch knew that he had done what he had tried to do. He had made his point. The spark had been struck and not too soon. He was satisfied. They would no doubt meet again, as she hoped. Torquil stepped forward and took Betty by the hand. He held it up with an air and, stooping over it, he kissed it.

"*Au revoir, duchesse*," he said.

Betty laughed loudly and said: "For goodness' sake don't do that or I shall come all over girlish. You make me think of Umberto. That was the sort of thing he used to do. The dirty dog!"

They moved off towards the front door, where they found Jasper waiting in the Ford and racing its engine feverishly. Torquil and Joanna climbed into the back of the car. Jasper started off without any warning and they were flung back violently against the seat. Before they disappeared down the drive Joanna turned and waved.

Zouch and Betty watched them go away round the bend and then turned back to the hall. There they found Mary, who said:

"Everyone has gone now, haven't they?"

Betty said: "Yes. And what do you think? I've just caught this young man getting off with Joanna Brandon under the stairs."

"Oh, come," said Zouch, "it wasn't as bad as that. I spoke to her for a few minutes but as you had introduced us it was the least I could do out of politeness."

"But why were you sitting under the stairs?" said Mary. She seemed half amused and half annoyed by what her sister had said.

"We weren't. Young Fosdick got us there for some reason or other."

"But he said that he found you there," Betty said. "This gets more and more suspicious."

Zouch said: "Well, he must have got muddled. And anyway I won't have either of you tease me any more. It isn't fair, two to one."

Inwardly he cursed Betty for thinking the incident a joke and Mary, when she was told about it, for thinking that it was not one. He saw that as usual it would be better to be careful as for some years now he had found being good to be almost out of the question. Mary said:

"Let's have some tea now, anyway, whatever they were doing."

Later, when they were having tea, Betty, who, having had any one subject fixed in her mind, found it difficult to turn at once to another, said:

"I must say Joanna was looking very pretty at the rehearsal, didn't you think, Mother?"

Mrs. Passenger looked up. She was as usual a little far

away and she had been having difficulty with Mr. Petal, who had grandiose ideas about how a pageant should be run. She said:

"Joanna Brandon?"

"Yes."

Mrs. Passenger thought for a long time as if she had never heard of anyone of that name. Mr. Petal and his views on pageant-economy hung above her like a grim shadow. She shook him off with an effort and said:

"I think Joanna is a very nice girl in many ways and I don't think she has a very good time. But I certainly shouldn't call her pretty. I don't want to be unkind but I should have thought that she was decidedly plain."

Betty said: "Mother, what an absolutely extraordinary thing to say. Why, I know people who would go mad about her. There are men I've met who would jump into the fire for her."

"But, Betty, you always seem to know such strange people. Why should they want to jump into the fire?"

"It's such an amusing face."

"But there is no colour in it at all. She's anæmic. I'm sure a tonic would do her good."

"I like that whiteness. And a lovely figure."

"My child, she is all skin and bone."

"Really, Mother, I can't understand you saying that," said Betty, who had become quite excited at the opposition to her views on Joanna's looks. "What do you think, Mary?" she said.

Mary was divided. She wanted terribly to have a modern taste in beauty. She said:

"I think Joanna looks quite nice sometimes. This afternoon, for instance. But I think she is rather a tiresome girl, as I've often told you."

Betty turned to Zouch.

"Anyway you agree that she looks lovely?" she said.

Zouch said: "You see it is rather difficult for me to give an opinion, being a painter. I think she might make a very interesting picture."

He tried to make his face alter when he spoke of his art without at the same time betraying too keen an interest in Joanna. Betty said:

"Well, you must be different from all the other painters I've ever met. And I've met a good few of them. They all held very definite views on female beauty."

Zouch said: "But you know a genuine artist never looks at anyone he wants to paint with the same eyes with which he would look at a beautiful woman he might meet in everyday life and want to—to say, get engaged to. He sees only the purely formal beauty, like that of a still life or a sunset."

And while he said this he really succeeded in dismissing from his mind the cavalcade of girls whom he had persuaded at one time or another to show him their appreciation of the drawings he had done of them. Mrs. Passenger raised her lorgnette. She said:

"Do you know, Mr. Zouch, I never knew that? How interesting. You must tell me about being an artist. What a fascinating life it must be."

FOUR

Major Fosdick was cleaning his guns in the drawing-room because it was the most comfortable room in the house. While he did this he brooded. He enjoyed cleaning his guns and he enjoyed brooding so that the afternoon was passing pleasantly enough and its charm was disturbed only by the presence of his wife, who sat opposite him, mending a flannel undergarment and making disjointed conversation about subjects in which he was not interested. She talked about the neighbours; about the pageant; about their children; about all the things which he had decided to put for the time being from his mind. Major Fosdick tried not to hear what she was saying. He thought about his youth and the years he had spent in Burma. Those had, in fact, been the days. Mrs. Fosdick said:

"Jasper has been doing well about his handicap."

"His handicap?"

"It's down again."

"It is?"

For a moment, in spite of himself, Major Fosdick thought about his elder son. A picture of Jasper appeared suddenly before him, looming up threateningly, like a figure in a nightmare. Jasper and his handicap. Jasper had so many handicaps that for the moment his father was unable to place which one it was to which his wife was referring. Mrs. Fosdick, all Hibernian, said:

"And didn't he go round yesterday in eighty-two?"

"Did he, did he?"

"That's better, isn't it?"

"Much better."

Thoughtfully, Major Fosdick dipped his rag into the oil again. Mentally, he compared himself as a young man to Jasper. Or as an old man, for that matter. Men like himself were not born any more now. *But now there are none like him, his like we'll never know.* Somebody had written that about Nelson. Or was it Wellington? Anyway it didn't make much odds. And then, *Something, something, something, there were giants in the land.* But there weren't any longer. Young men were different now, he thought. Perhaps it was just as well. Major Fosdick laughed silently to himself.

"Now what are you laughing at, George?"

"Nothing."

Mrs. Fosdick pursed her lips. She did not like her husband having jokes in which she had no share. It was a habit he was far too fond of. She had been disturbed lately, too, about his behaviour. He was getting even more secretive than he used to be. Just a little unbalanced, she thought. She said:

"I often think it might be a good thing for Jasper to get married. It would settle him down."

Major Fosdick polished away but did not answer. He thought, I'll give her a crack over the head in a minute. Mrs. Fosdick said:

"He's wild. It's the Irish strain in him. He's a bit of a Paddy. He gets that from me."

She smiled to herself, with pleasure and in retaliation. The setter, curled up on the turkey carpet, growled in his sleep, woke up suddenly, and began to turn round and round with violence, snorting at his tail.

"Shut up!" said Major Fosdick. "Shut up, you brute!"

He hoped that his wife would consider herself included

in this injunction, but Mrs. Fosdick pursued her train of thought.

"What do you think of Joanna Brandon?" she said.

"What do I think of her? What do you mean, what do I think of her? She seems a sensible sort of girl. Much like anyone else. What are you driving at? I wish you wouldn't disturb me. This is a very tricky business."

"Do you think that she would make Jasper happy?"

Major Fosdick put down the rook-rifle and the oil and the rag and the toothpick, with which he had been getting some dirt from under the sights, and said:

"What on earth do you mean, Veronica? Why should she *make him happy*? Isn't he happy already? He always seems very happy to me. What possible business is it of hers? Besides I don't know what you mean at all. It sounds to me a very funny way to talk."

"But don't you know that they are secretly engaged? She adores him."

Secretly engaged? Well of all the—— Major Fosdick took up his gun again. He said:

"Don't—talk—rot."

"Didn't you see how they went off together after lunch when she came here some Sundays ago?"

Major Fosdick only growled. Mrs. Fosdick said:

"There don't seem to be many nice girls round here. There is Mary Passenger, of course, but she and Jasper never seem to get on very well together. And then I expect the Passengers would make all sorts of difficulties about money. The Braby girls are nice, but I know Jasper. He would want something more distinguished. He has such high ideals, you know. Of course it would be very nice for a lot of reasons if he did marry Mary Passenger."

"He might be able to ram some sense into that father of hers. Teach him not to be so selfish about his shooting."

"But it is quite out of the question I'm afraid. It would never be arranged. There are too many difficulties in the way."

"Passenger ought to have learnt some sense, some knowledge of the world, at his age."

"So that is why I was thinking of Joanna."

Major Fosdick gave it up. His wife was impossible. What was the good of talking to someone like that? At this moment Torquil came into the room and became involved with his mother in a conversation about the pageant and Major Fosdick was left in peace. He engaged himself once more with his own thoughts. These became more and more wild as time wore on and at last his head seemed wholly filled with the phantoms he had conjured up and it buzzed fearfully with the sound of strange music. But all the time he polished his guns and smiled gently to himself as if he were thinking of nothing more startling than pig-sticking or quiet afternoons spent in North Copse.

Joanna sat in the garden and tried to read *War and Peace*, because she had seen somewhere, in some paper, that it was one of the great books of the world. But she did not make much headway reading it. She found difficulty in following the narrative and there were the accustomed distractions of reading in the open air, the flight of birds and distant noises in the town to which the stillness of afternoon gave some fugitive meaning. In a street near-by she could hear the Orphans playing their organ. And she thought a certain amount about Zouch and wondered what sort of a young man he really was. To this preoccupation were added the fitful appearances of Mrs. Dadds, who had embarked on a series of self-imposed excursions which took her backwards and forwards from the summer-house and within a few yards of Joanna's chair. Mrs. Dadds's attitude towards the problem of human relationships made it out of the question that she should pass this point without making at least one comment on current affairs or remark on life of more or less general application.

To hear Mrs. Dadds talk it would have been excusable to have supposed that she had been in the service of the Brandon family for several generations or alternatively that she had been employed by some ducal house for an immense number of years and had taken on her present situation merely as a favour to the Brandons. Her systematically dishevelled hair was against her, certainly, and also the irregularity of her front teeth, several of which were gone for good, but whatever conspicuous imperfections of this kind she might possess she made up for without effort by the assurance of her behaviour.

She had appeared some years before in answer to an advertisement in the local paper. Mrs. Brandon found difficulty in keeping servants and so in spite of her manifestly forged references and her appearance, which on her first entry into the Brandons' house touched almost its highest peak of oddity, she was engaged. Later, she and Mrs. Brandon became great cronies and would talk to each other endlessly. Neither of them made any effort to listen to what the other was saying, so that often they would speak for hours together on two entirely different subjects. However, they respected each other's egos according to their own lights and although Mrs. Brandon was in many ways an exigent mistress and Mrs. Dadds was congenitally lazy, it all worked pretty well. Mrs. Brandon was sometimes behindhand in paying wages and Mrs. Dadds was in the habit of appropriating any little odds and ends left lying about which happened to take her fancy. It was, in short, an effective compromise.

Standing in the middle of the lawn on this summer after-

noon Mrs. Dadds was seen to the fullest advantage. Nothing
was missing to complete the inelegance of her appearance.
Her petticoat was coming down at the back and there was a
smudge of lampblack on her forehead. When she stood still
her body leant always a little to the right.

"I wonder you don't get tired of reading all day long,
Miss Joanna."

Joanna said: "I do."

She implied by her tone that the tedium of reading was
incomparably less than that of talking to Mrs. Dadds. The
afternoon was warm and she wished that the print of her
book was larger and the book itself less heavy to hold. Mrs.
Dadds said:

"My husband was a great reader. He'd read anything
that came his way. I had no patience with him. I used to
say to him, 'If you don't put that book down this minute,
you'll find me after you.'"

"What did he say to that?"

"What did he say?" said Mrs. Dadds.

She paused in contemplation, savouring in her mind what
her husband had said, like the remembrance of some rare
and piquant taste that she would perhaps never have an
opportunity of enjoying again. She said:

"What did he say, Miss Joanna? If I told you some of the
things he used to say to me, your mother would turn me
out of the house. The foul-mouthed brute!"

"What sort of things?"

Joanna wondered whether the end of the speech was intended to apply to her mother or to Mrs. Dadds's husband.
Anyway it did not much matter. She felt that this would
be a good opportunity for learning about married life, as
she was quite interested in this as a subject. But Mrs. Dadds
only shook her head and said:

"The filthy beast!"

On the other side of the house the bell, an old ship's bell that hung on a bracket outside the front door, clanged. Mrs. Dadds started involuntarily, but she recovered herself almost at once and said:

"Well, they say when you're married your troubles begin, and when they say that they speak the truth. The men, they're the same the whole lot of them. They just want one thing and when you've given them that they're finished with you. All you're good for is to slave and slave and slave, keeping them comfortable, wearing your flesh to the bone. I often used to tell that to that good-for-nothing husband of mine."

"Hadn't you better see who that is at the front door?"

"I used to say to him, 'I suppose you expect to live in the lap of luxury while I wait on you hand and foot? You ought to go to India where you could sit in the sun all day long and be fanned by the blacks. That's all you're good for.'"

"If it is Mr. Jasper Fosdick," said Joanna, "tell him I'm out."

The bell pealed again and, unmooring herself from her subject, Mrs. Dadds moved off at her leisure in the direction of the house. Over her shoulder she said:

"You'll remember what I've said when the time comes for you to get married, Miss Joanna."

Joanna went on with her reading. She sincerely wished that she was married. But not to Jasper. She felt that she would prefer to marry almost anyone to Jasper. She was confident that it was he who had come to pay a call. It was earlier in the afternoon than his usual time for calling but he had not been to see her for so long that he was due any day now and at any moment. She turned over the page, came to the end of a chapter and shut the book, leaning back in her chair and looking up towards the roofs on the other side of the garden wall above which some rooks were flying in circles. Mrs. Dadds advanced again from the direction of the house. She approached the deck-chair.

"A young gentleman to see you, miss."

"Mr. Fosdick? Either of them?"

"No, miss."

"Who is it?"

"Never seen him before."

"What is his name?"

"Couldn't catch his name."

"But who can he be?"

"He's got a beard. He says you know him, Miss Joanna."

"Oh, he's got a beard, has he?" said Joanna. She dropped *War and Peace* on the ground beside her. "Was his name Zouch?" she said.

"Something like that."

"And he wants to see me?"

"That's what he said."

"Well bring him out here. And bring another deck-chair."

Mrs. Dadds looked surprised. Hurt, almost. It was as if Joanna had let her down in some way by knowing the caller. It was like a breach of confidence. She said, rather resentfully:

"Then you do know him, Miss Joanna?"

"Yes. Of course I do. He is staying at Passenger. Go and show him in now. He mustn't be kept waiting any longer."

Mrs. Dadds went away to fetch Zouch, but with a lack of conviction. Joanna touched her hair and took up her book again and pretended to read. In a few seconds she felt that Zouch was coming towards her across the lawn. When she thought that he was fairly near she looked up and was intending to say something appropriate from her chair when she lost her head and, getting up again, went to meet him. She had meant to say something rather dignified like 'How nice to see you unexpectedly like this,' or, 'Fancy your remembering the name of our house,' but when it came to the point she said, a little breathlessly :

"Do you want to see me?"

When he was a couple of yards off Zouch had stopped, and he stood there looking at her. Dramatically, he took hold of the end of his beard with his left hand and he stood looking at Joanna for quite a long time. He was dressed with great care and was feeling at the top of his form.

"Yes," he said, "I want to see you."

In the background Mrs. Dadds came staggering out of the house, carrying in the most difficult manner possible an open deck-chair. She dropped this at Zouch's feet, by a curious sleight of hand contriving to turn it inside out. She closed with the chair, and half-falling on the ground, began to grapple with it.

"Leave it," said Joanna. "We'll put it right somehow."

"That always happens, miss, with these chairs."

"No, no. Leave it. We can do it."

It took some time but in the end the chair was arranged for use, and reluctantly Mrs. Dadds left them together. Zouch sat down. He said :

"I was passing through the town and I thought that I should very much like to see you again. I hope you don't mind my calling on you suddenly like this?"

"Of course not. It's awfully nice of you to remember me."

Zouch said : "I felt I absolutely must see you again. As soon as possible."

Joanna laughed. She had begun to feel tremendously excited. Something was happening at last. She must keep her head.

"But how nice of you to say so," she said.

She saw that he was excited too. She still held *War and Peace* in her hand. She was holding it so tightly that she knew that the red from its cover must be coming off on to her palm.

"What are you reading?" Zouch said.

He put his arm across one of hers and tipped up the book slightly so that he could see the chapter heading. The print was small and it was several seconds before he could read it and all the time he let his arm lie across hers and rest on her knee with some of his weight behind it so that Joanna felt herself trembling a little at the contact of her body with his.

She made an effort and said:

"Have you read it?"

She wondered if her voice sounded to him, as it sounded to herself, a thousand miles away. Zouch said:

"No. It is too long."

And then from sheer nervous tension she stood up again. Zouch got up too and took her by the arm. Inwardly she thought how her mother would be asleep at this time in the afternoon and also she thought how little she cared if Mrs. Dadds was watching them from the dining-room window. So people really felt like this. It was all true, those violent emotions that were described in books.

"Let's walk about," he said. "I came to tell you that I was in love with you."

"Did you?"

"Yes."

"But I am in love with you," she said.

"Are you?"

"Yes. I am in love with you."

When, later in the summer-house, they discussed the matter, she told him that she had been in love with him from the moment that she had seen him for the first time, when he had come into the church and had sat with the Passengers in their pew. She had been in love with him since then, she said, which was not entirely true because at first she had thought about him only with a sort of amiable curiosity. All the same his technique in love-making frightened her a little, because she was familiar only with the attacks of ungainly young men who had had a glass too much of champagne at hunt-ball suppers or even Major Fosdick, who had become very arch one Christmas under a sprig of mistletoe in the town hall. But with Zouch all this seemed quite different and she was surprised when at last it occurred to her to look at her watch to find how late they were for tea. It was past five o'clock. Zouch himself was aware that he must still be careful and he behaved with what he considered great restraint. She lifted her head from his shoulder and said:

"We must go and have some tea now. My mother will wonder what has happened to me. She is more or less an invalid, you know."

"I ought to be getting back to Passenger."

"Oh, do stay."

"I'm not sure that I ought to."

"Oh, you must."

"All right then."

All the time he had intended to stay. The Passengers had gone to see some relations who lived near and who were avowedly too boring to inflict on guests. Zouch had been told this by Betty and he was warned that if he came with them it was at his own risk. He had said, therefore, that he would go off by himself and do some painting, and it was only after the car had driven away that it had occurred to him that now would be an excellent opportunity to pay a call on Joanna. He had found that since seeing her he had thought of nothing else. He was quite used to feeling that about women but it surprised him that he would feel like this towards a girl of Joanna's type and it was an inconvenient thing to happen when one was staying with people.

They found Mrs. Brandon, who had already finished her tea, lying on the sofa. She showed no surprise at seeing Zouch and as usual she rose admirably to the occasion. She did not, in fact, mind a chance visitor, more especially someone who did not live permanently in the neighbourhood and in any case she had so perfected her talent for allowing no part of herself to touch the outer world that she was almost immune even from the contacts of local people who might have known her for many years. However she preferred to run no risks in this matter and local callers were few and far between.

"And so you live in London," she said to Zouch. "Dear old London. I often wish that I could see it again. How different it must look now that there are no more hansom cabs. Not that one was ever supposed to go in them, though I must admit that I did more than once when I was a girl. I simply couldn't resist it. But then I was headstrong when I was younger. No one could manage me at all. But those days are all gone now. And I don't expect London is the same at all either."

Zouch said that he was sure that Mrs. Brandon would find the place changed out of all recognition. Somewhere behind those ruins lying on the sofa he could see traces of Joanna. It was a sobering thought and as such he put it from his mind. To-day he felt that for a short time he might permit himself escape from the sphere of sobering influences. He glanced round him at the room he was sitting in. This was uniformly disagreeable in arrangement and contained several pieces of furniture of quite grotesque ugliness. He noticed on the mantelpiece some medals on red velvet in a small glass case. While he looked about him Spot and Ranger sniffed doubtfully at his trouser-legs. Mrs. Brandon said:

"So you are staying at Passenger. What a lovely house it is, don't you think? The ballroom is a beautiful room. What a pity they can't afford to keep it up better. But it is the same all over the country. All the old places falling down or being sold. And how is Vernon Passenger? I used to know him so well and now I hardly ever see him. You see I am tied to my room. One misses so much by being an old crock. But Joanna goes up there sometimes, don't you, darling?"

"I met Mr. Zouch up there."

"But Passenger has changed too, like everything else," Mrs. Brandon said. "It can't be as it was in the old days."

"Has it?"

"Terribly."

"You know Mr. Zouch is an artist," said Joanna.

She saw that her mother was heading for her favourite subject, the shortcomings of Mrs. Passenger, and she judged it safer to change the topic of conversation. As soon as she had said this she regretted it. Art was another of Mrs. Brandon's favourite subjects.

"Are you really? But, of course that is why you have come to this part of the country. There is beauty everywhere. The town is simply full of picturesque bits. You must see the sunsets we get over the canal. This is something that you can really look forward to."

"I shall take care not to miss them."

"Have you ever thought what a strange thing beauty is, Mr. Zouch? It is like some little shell that has been washed up by the waves and left on the sand of the seashore where any wanderer may pick it up and at any moment the waves may return and wash it back again and it is taken from us almost before we know that we have a chance to snatch it up and keep it for our own."

"Yes, absolutely," said Zouch.

The simile seemed familiar, somehow, but for the moment he was unable to place the work from which Mrs. Brandon had selected it. He tried to memorise it for his own use in the future.

"If you are interested in painting," said Mrs. Brandon, "look at that picture there. And that one there."

Zouch looked at them and, as comment was out of the question, he made an appreciative face and nodded heavily several times.

"I often look at those two pictures," said Mrs. Brandon. "That is one of the few pleasures I have left. But it is a very keen one. My love of beauty is almost all that remains to me. That and my sense of humour."

Later when it was time for him to go back to Passenger, Joanna went with him as far as the front door. In the hall he took her by the wrists. She drew back a little.

"Why do you do that?" he said.

She did not answer. Still holding her hands, he said:

"When am I going to see you again?"

"Any time. Whenever you like. Whenever you can. You can always see me."

"Will there be another rehearsal soon?"

"Yes. And Torquil Fosdick is giving a cocktail-party. You must come to that. Will you come to that?"

"I haven't been asked yet."

"But you will be asked. You must come. Don't let Mary Passenger prevent you from coming."

"But why should she?"

"Oh, I don't know. She might say she didn't want to go herself and try and stop you from going because of that. But Betty will certainly be there."

D

"All right. I'll be there too."

She avoided his mouth and the kiss landed somewhere near her ear. But it was like that sometimes at the beginning, he thought. He went away after that, down the stone path that led to the gate. He kissed his hand to her as he shut the gate and Joanna waved back. Then she returned along the passage. She went slowly into the room where they had been having tea and shut the door behind her. Mrs. Brandon was reading her book again.

"What a strange young man, darling."

"Isn't he?"

"I wonder where the Passengers found him?"

"They know all sorts of people."

"Is he a friend of Betty Passenger's then? She knows a lot of artists, I believe. In fact, they say she doesn't mind who she goes about with."

"No; Mary, I think."

"His beard does look funny, doesn't it?"

"Oh, I don't know. You quite often see people with beards."

"Not in the country, darling. I never do."

"But you don't go out much."

"I'm not able to, Joanna. As you know my health doesn't allow me to. I'm just a poor old invalid. I can only lie here and dream. And Joanna—wait a moment—when you pass the dining-room mix mother a whisky-and-soda and bring it to her before you go upstairs."

Mr. Passenger came out of Jeudwine's, the saddler's, where he had been paying a bill, and walked across the broad stretch of High Street opposite the Fox and Hounds. After promising his wife that he would go with her and his daughters to visit their irksome relatives, he had said at the last moment that he could not face them, having decided on impulse that it would be preferable to spend the afternoon pottering round the town and aggravating some of his *bêtes noires* among the local tradesmen. He had been doing this with satisfactory results and he was now on his way home. There was always a chance that Major Fosdick might be about the streets at this time of day, in which case the question of North Copse might profitably be reopened.

Mr. Passenger walked along the middle of the empty High Street, feeling his moustache and swinging his thick walking-stick, which had a bone handle and a gold band round it with an inscription on it from the local boy scouts, who had presented it to him. He felt that he had had a thoroughly gratifying afternoon and he was congratulating himself on having avoided several hours of shouting at old Lady Llanstephan, who thought that the war was still on and always confused him with his uncle who had died of apoplexy at King Edward's coronation at which he had been assisting in some subordinate capacity. Mr. Passenger was so engrossed in his reflections that he did not notice that Zouch was coming towards him, also walking in the middle of the road. As Zouch himself was occupied with thoughts of Joanna he did not see Mr. Passenger and it was an unpleasant surprise for both of them when they found themselves almost face to face. Mr. Passenger recovered himself first and said:

"Well? Did you discover anything worth painting?"

Zouch had forgotten the original object of his walk but he pulled himself together and said that he had done no work that afternoon, although he had seen several suitable subjects which he hoped to tackle in the near future. Mr. Passenger grunted. Both saw at once that they would have to walk back to Passenger together. Mr. Passenger said:

"On your way back now, I expect?"

"Yes."

"We might go across the fields. It's longer but less dusty than the road."

They walked along in silence out of the town and up the hill. Turning off to the right at the signpost, they went along a sandy road and over a stile which stood at the end of the footpath leading across the fields.

"Where did you go?" said Mr. Passenger.

He suspected that Zouch had come into the town to buy himself a drink at the Fox and Hounds before returning to Passenger. He was glad to think that he might have defeated this object, because he had already begun to dislike Zouch a great deal. He felt that the absence of his daughters put him in a stronger position than that in which he usually found himself in his own house. He looked at Zouch searchingly to overawe him. Zouch described in vague terms the walk he was supposed to have taken. They tramped on through the tufts of grass. Mr. Passenger said:

"Ah, yes. You went round by North Copse. Did you see anything of that stupid old Fosdick? He is usually hanging about there."

"No," said Zouch. "What does he do there."

He thought it might be worth his while to make a more searching study of local conditions. Knowledge was power, he remembered having read somewhere.

"He shoots my birds whenever he can," said Mr. Passenger. "Or, if it makes it any clearer to you to put it that way, he poaches. Still, it's no use grumbling. He hires the place. He's got it on a long lease. I've tried to buy him out and he won't hear of it, so there it is."

They approached some trees and entered a small wood. On the other side of the wood the grass sloped down to a gap in the hedge. In the distance Zouch could hear a droning noise like the sound of machinery a long way off.

"That was last year I was speaking of," said Mr. Passenger. "The year before that the birds were so wild that there was nothing to be done with them at all. Between you and me I shouldn't be surprised to meet old Fosdick one of these days with a parcel of bran and sultanas under his arm. I wish I could catch him red-handed. He'd hear something then."

Feeling that the intrinsic interest of the subject was becoming submerged by technicalities that held little profit for the general public, Zouch decided to change it and so he said:

"What is the fishing like round here?" And added, drawing a bow at a venture, "It should be good."

Mr. Passenger did not immediately answer. He was holding back some brambles so that they could pass into the next field. While he did this he stopped and listened. The noise which they had heard a few seconds before was becoming louder and now it could be recognised as the voices of persons singing. As Mr. Passenger paused, discordant chantings rasped towards them through the soft country air. All at once the afternoon was made hideous by an increasing volume of inharmonious sound.

"What is that?" Mr. Passenger said.

"What can it be?"

They went through the brambles, into the next field. From the gate opposite figures advanced across the plough. As they came nearer the figures revealed themselves as men and women, though which were which it was at first not easy to infer as both were dressed in shorts and bright-coloured shirts without distinction as to sex. One at least had side-whiskers and one of the more uncompromising female members of the party wore plus-fours. The words which they were singing could now be distinguished.

Boney was a warrior!
Ho! Hi! Ho!

Mr. Passenger said: "Here, I say, what's all this?"

"Hikers."

"Hikers?" said Mr. Passenger. "*Hikaz?*"

The word was evidently unfamiliar to him and he pronounced it as if it belonged to some oriental language. But Zouch did not embark on an explanation of its meaning or derivation. He was wondering whether anything so horrible could be true. Yet the man in the green shirt was indeed Fischbein; and the dwarfish girl in horn-rimmed spectacles was Fischbein's girl. There was no doubt about it. They walked before him in the flesh. He was not stumbling through a nightmare. It was really a little too much. Fischbein. His girl. Zouch's brain reeled. Was it for this, he wondered, that people spoke reverently of the duty to preserve rural England? Was there no power to protect these lovely regions from defilement by Fischbein and his filthy loves. The noise by now had become deafening. It was an occasion that called for diplomatic handling. Here the superman touch would not come amiss. Zouch decided to get his speech in first. He said:

"You know it's an extraordinary thing but I believe that I know one of those people. He is a journalist and a remarkably clever fellow in his way. Rather eccentric, you know, but he has written one or two very good things in his time. He is a tremendous walker too. He often says that he simply can't do without exercise. He thinks nothing of walking twenty or thirty miles in a day."

"Really?"

Mr. Passenger's eyes remained fixed upon the oncoming horde. He was not listening.

"An amazing fellow," said Zouch. "In that way."

Fischbein and his party drew nearer. Zouch nerved himself for Fischbein's greeting. The hikers were advancing in diamond formation, organised in depth. Fischbein's recognition came with piercing suddenness. He gave a yell and shouted :

"Why if it isn't that old devil, Zouch! Whoopee!"

"Hallo," said Zouch, with restraint. "Hallo, Hetty. Fancy meeting both of you here."

Fischbein stood in front of Zouch with his hands on his hips. He had a grey face, full of folds and swellings of loose flesh, like a piece of bad realistic sculpture. In everyday life he had a permanent but very humble position on the staff of a serious little weekly paper and he had been known to augment his income by ghosting for illiterate memoir writers.

"Well, I don't know so much about that," he said, in his fruity, old-time comedian voice. "I don't know so much about that. After all Hetty and I do this most week-ends during the summer when it's fine, but I didn't know that you were ever to be found so far west of the King's Road, Chelsea. Where are you staying?"

"Near here," said Zouch, momentarily shaken by the force of Fischbein's onslaught.

"This is Mr. Fischbein," he said to Mr. Passenger, in order to gain time.

"How do you do," said Mr. Passenger, looking at Fischbein with a sort of horrified fascination.

"Delighted I'm sure," said Fischbein. "This is Hetty. Here, Hetty, come and be introduced. Don't be shy. Where did you say you were staying?"

Behind him, Zouch heard Mr. Passenger ask Hetty whether she had walked far that day, and Hetty reply that she would have been farther if her shorts had not been so tight. The rest of the hikers had disappeared into the woods to the accompaniment of shouts of "*Ho! Hi! Ho!*" which were now growing fainter. Zouch said, in answer to Fischbein's question:

"In a house over there. You can't see it from where we are standing. It is some little way from here."

"But the only house for miles in that direction is Passenger Court. We have just come that way. You don't mean to tell me that you are staying at Passenger Court?"

Fischbein's face expressed amusement rather than respect or approval. Mr. Passenger was still occupied with Hetty. He was giving her a warning against the breaking down of hedges. Zouch said:

"Yes. As a matter of fact I am."

"You can't be."

"I repeat that I am."

It looked as if he would be able to keep Mr. Passenger's identity secret. That was important. Mr. Passenger continued to enlarge on the laws of trespass and he would not hear what Fischbein was saying. As long as Hetty did not try to vamp him, no great harm could be done. Even that would be better than that he should join in Zouch's conversation with Fischbein.

"But how on earth did you get there?" Fishbein said. "Are you staying with the housekeeper or something like that? Or are you having a little game with one of the housemaids? Don't tell me you were asked there by the Passengers?"

"Yes."

"Phew! Is Bella with you?"

"No," said Zouch, through his teeth.

"Oh, well," said Fischbein. "I suppose one can't have everything on these occasions. Anyway it's rather jolly to feel that one is on one's own once in a while. We are calling a halt in the town, as it happens. Why don't you come down to the local about half-past seven and have a drink?"

"I can't."

"Why not?"

Zouch said: "It is rather a long story. I can't go into it all now but the fact remains that I can't. I'm afraid it is quite impossible. I'm sorry."

"That's all right," said Fischbein. "I don't expect it will be long before we meet again and we can have one then. I suppose I shall have to be catching up the rest of them now."

He pointed to the wood into which the remainder of his party had disappeared, and through which their singing could now scarcely be heard.

"Good-bye."

"Ta-ta," said Fischbein. "Come along, Hetty."

He waved to Mr. Passenger and in a few moments he and Hetty were also lost among the trees. Mr. Passenger stood, rooted to the spot. Zouch said:

"It's really amazing what a clever fellow that is. You'd never think it just to meet him."

Mr. Passenger said: "What was he wearing on his head? I could not make out. But you were asking about the fishing round here. I will tell you. Some of it is not bad at all. Quite good, in fact. Quite good."

The rest of the Passenger family had returned from their visit and Mary was amusing herself by sticking snapshots into her album, while Betty, leaning over the back of the sofa, watched her do this. The sisters were alone together in the room. Mary held up one of the photographs. She said:

"Did you ever see anything like Charles Kettleby in this?"

"Where was it taken?"

"At Blackladies when I was there last summer. Now give me the scissors. I'm going to cut out that odious little Hester Manningham before I stick it in."

"Here's another of Charles Kettleby. You know he's rather attractive in a way. Of course he's being silly here. You know Angela absolutely adored him for years."

"Now the paste."

Betty said: "Of course I used to know Charles Kettleby years and years and years ago. What I always hated about him was the way he would go on ragging all the time. He never knows when to stop. Besides he gets so rough. Once I met him at a dance in Ireland and he nearly broke my leg. What is it you want now? The scissors again?"

"Charles is rather too much really."

"He's rather like what Jasper Fosdick might have been if he was a human being."

Mary laughed. She cut out a photograph of herself sitting on some stairs between two young men, one of whom, from being too near the flashlight, appeared to have had half his face blown away. She picked up her fountain-pen and wrote the name and the date of the dance underneath the picture. Betty said:

"Oh and talking of the Fosdicks, we've been asked by Torquil to go to a cocktail-party that he is giving. It is going to be some time next week."

"A cocktail-party. How extraordinary. At their house?"

"At the Fox and Hounds."

"We can't possibly go. It would be too awful for words."

"I think we ought to go. It might be rather fun."

"It couldn't possibly be."

"Well I said that we would both go anyway. Do back me up. Your boy-friend will enjoy it too."

"Don't call him that, Betty. You make me feel quite ill.

I suppose we've got to go there if you've said that we are going but I'd much rather not."

"It won't be as bad as that. I think it might be rather fun."

Mary made a face. Lately she had not been at her best. Without having any clear idea as to what it was that she wanted, she had begun to feel dissatisfied all day long. In the past when she had been attacked by depression she had dreamed about a tall husband with a country house that was a manageable size and a modern flat not too far from Berkeley Square. But all that had begun to seem unreal, insipid somehow, and the thought of this husband of her imagination, leaning back on his shooting-stick at Hawthorn Hill with his bowler tilted over his eyes and his field-glasses half raised as together they watched the horses coming over the last jump, in her present mood, merely made her feel exhausted. Somehow it did not seem any longer to be what she wanted. And even if it had been what she wanted, there were no signs of such a person putting in an appearance. Men proposed to her sometimes but there was always something wrong about them so that looking back on these proposals they seemed to her little better than a lot of jokes in rather bad taste. As husbands all these men were quite out of the question and yet one by one the girls who had been débutantes at the same time as herself were getting married and even divorced. She wondered if she were being left on the shelf.

She closed her photograph album.

"I'm tired of these beastly photographs," she said. "And how awful it was this afternoon. I had to tell cousin Judith five times that I didn't play bridge. I'm never going to allow myself to be dragged over there again."

"I like going there," Betty said. "It makes me feel such

a bad woman. I also enjoy the sensation so much of their not liking me being there. I always pray that someone whom they think important will come in and be shocked by me."

"I should have thought that you were used to shocking people by this time."

"It's a thing I never get tired of."

Mary said: "Well I sometimes get tired of your doing it."

There were times when her sister got on her nerves. She disapproved of the life which Betty had led and yet at the same time she had begun to envy certain features of it. She had never questioned Betty about her marriage and now when the details of it had begun to interest her it seemed to be too late. She did not know where to begin. And besides Betty's point of view was so different from her own that any experiences which Betty might have had seemed remote from anything that could possibly happen to herself. She was still thinking about these matters when Zouch and Mr. Passenger came into the room.

"Hallo, Father," said Betty. "What sort of an afternoon did you have?"

"Well. Tell me about yourselves first," said Mr. Passenger. "How were they all?"

"Worse than ever," Betty said. "Far worse."

Mr. Passenger said: "I knew that they would be. How very fortunate that I did not come with you. Did they ask after me?"

"No."

"They didn't?"

"You weren't mentioned."

"Do you mean that no one asked after me?"

"No one."

"Not even cousin Judith?"

"No."

"Really," said Mr. Passenger. "And then they say that blood is thicker than water. They know perfectly well that I have had hay-fever. I made your mother write and tell them so. And yet they don't enquire after me. I shall certainly never go over there again."

"Uncle Frederick's leg has been bad again."

"All imagination. Imagination and lack of exercise."

Mr. Passenger shook his head moodily.

"All your mother's family are just the same," he said. "Hopelessly selfish."

"And where have you been, Father?"

"I went to the town. I looked in at Jeudwine's to see about repairing the panel of that saddle of Mary's. And then I met this young man and we walked back across the fields." And Mr. Passenger added rather spitefully: "Where we met some friends of his."

Having shot this arrow into the air, Mr. Passenger went away. He was preparing, in the secrecy of his own room, a short history of the manor on which Passenger was built and he intended to make a few notes on this work before it was time for dinner. When he had gone, Mary said:

"Who can you have met coming across the fields?"

In her own mind she wondered suddenly if it had been Joanna Brandon. She thought of this all at once, not knowing why she did so except that she thought of Joanna as the only person in the neighbourhood whom Zouch knew.

"Oh, no one special," Zouch said. "Just a man, a journalist. Rather an eccentric sort of person. But clever, you know."

With Fischbein at a safe distance he felt that he could afford to be patronising. He said:

"I hope your father wasn't shocked by his appearance. He looked very odd, I'm afraid."

"Oh, father doesn't care what anyone looks like," said Mary. "Look at the way he dresses himself."

Mary was not thinking about what she was saying so much as of the strange feeling of relief that she was experiencing on learning that it was not Joanna whom he had met. She was unaccustomed to analysing her thoughts but at the same time she was conscious of a distinct sense of irritation that she should find herself thinking of Joanna at all in connection with Zouch.

"And what have you been doing?" said Zouch, who was not anxious to be cross-questioned too fully as to how he had spent his own afternoon.

"Well we went on this awful visit and when we came back I began to stick in photographs. But I got tired of it, so I stopped just before you came in."

"May I see some of the photographs?"

"Yes, of course. I think I will go on now. Will you help me cut some of them out?"

"What's happening here?"

"That's me and someone called Charles Kettleby."

Zouch sat down on the sofa beside Mary who collected the pile of photographs between them and picked out some to show him. Betty, who was still holding the scissors in her hand, put them down on the table. She said:

"If you want me, though I see no reason why you should, I shall be in the library playing the gramophone. And by the way, we have all been asked to a cocktail-party. What do you think of that? You see the country is really very gay. It is not dull at all as people like you, who come down from London, suppose."

"Whose cocktail-party?"

"Torquil Fosdick's. At the Fox and Hounds."

Mary said: "I warn you it will be simply awful. I really don't think I can go, Betty. Why don't you go alone if you really want to." She turned to Zouch and said: "I'm sure you don't really want to go either, do you? You're only being polite. You must go to all the cocktail-parties you want in London."

Zouch said: "You know, just out of curiosity, I should rather like to go. Will it really be as bad as all that?"

Mary said: "It will be too awful for words. Torquil's so tiresome."

Betty said: "Well you've both of you got to go anyway, because I've accepted for both of you, and I won't have a word against Torquil who is quite the sweetest boy who ever happened."

She left them together on the sofa. They stuck in photographs until dinner-time. Mary had begun to feel quite happy again. Zouch was pleased with himself too. It had been a good day. Except for Fischbein.

FIVE

Mrs. Passenger, who was thinking about the pageant and the cottage hospital and the best place to get bath-salts, walked across the lawn in the direction of Capes the gardener. She stopped to have a look at the monkey-puzzles on the way. It was a fine morning and there was an exhilarating feeling of freshness in the air. Capes was on all fours by one of the flower-beds, tying aluminium labels on to the stalks of some withered shrubs. Mrs. Passenger came close up to him before he saw her. When he looked round at last he got up laboriously from the ground and stood with his eyes fixed on her while he wiped his hands on the seat of his trousers.

"Good morning, Capes."

"Good morning, m'lady."

This was a danger-signal. Capes only called Mrs. Passenger that when he was in a bad temper. It was a warning for her to keep her distance. The running up of the Jolly Roger. Mrs. Passenger knew this and proceeded cautiously. There were several things which she intended to say.

"What a beautiful morning it is."

"Yes, m'lady."

"I want to speak to you, Capes, about staking the gladioli. You know it is very important to stake them early if the flowers are to do well. I think that in past years they may have been left a little late."

Capes watched Mrs. Passenger with profound melancholy. He continued his self-massage, turning his eyes to the ground. At the same time he gave a sort of groan to himself. Mrs. Passenger said :

"And then there was another thing. The old wood wants cutting away from the flowered-out ramblers. The new wood must be given every opportunity of growing."

"Yes, m'lady."

"Will you see to that?"

"Very good, m'lady."

Mrs. Passenger paused. There was something else too. What was it? She was thinking how lovely a morning it was and how nice the house looked from this part of the garden. She must make arrangements to have it photographed from this spot. *Country Life* might be interested. If they ever wanted to sell the place it was always as well to have something of that kind to show prospective buyers.

"Oh, yes. About the kitchen garden. The cauliflowers. Have you tried working salt into the soil in showery weather?"

Capes shook his head. He looked more wretched than ever.

"Tried it aforetime," he said, becoming all at once a stage peasant, a line of defence he sometimes took up when Mr. or Mrs. Passenger became too exigent.

"It works wonders with the heads."

"Yes, m'lady."

"Lady Llanstephan was telling me about it when we were over there the other day."

"She was, ma'am?"

"She said they had found it very successful."

Zouch, who had been strolling round the garden to make a break in the morning's work, which had consisted in doing some drawings of Betty's head, came through the trees. Mrs. Passenger, absorbed in her own thoughts, watched him walking towards her. Capes had had enough.

He knelt down at Mrs. Passenger's feet as if he were about to ask her to run away with him. He did not actually continue the work he was attending to, but his position made it clear to Mrs. Passenger that he considered that she was wasting his time.

"I thought I would mention these things to you."

"Very good, ma'am."

"You can see about them then."

"Yes, ma'am."

Mrs. Passenger inspected the shrubs through her lorgnette. Capes took the opportunity to shift his position a little and to return to the aluminium labels. Zouch reached the place where they were standing. He joined Mrs. Passenger in her examination of the thrubs. Mrs. Passenger said:

"Are you interested in gardens, Mr. Zouch?"

"Yes," said Zouch cautiously, "I am."

"But they take up so much time."

Zouch agreed that they did. This was the first time since his stay that he had found himself alone with Mrs. Passenger and he was anxious to make as good an impression as possible.

"Come with me," Mrs. Passenger said, "and I will show you some of this garden."

They left Capes, by this time almost prone on the ground, and walked back across the lawn. Zouch was in a receptive mood. In retrospect the encounter with Fischbein had produced a strong effect upon him. He had made up his mind to change his way of life. Fischbein and all he stood for was to be a thing of the past. Mrs. Passenger and the garden symbolised a dignified and more successful future. Mrs. Passenger said:

"I hear that you are going to paint a picture of my granddaughter."

"Yes. Bianca has promised to sit for me. I am looking forward to it very much."

"She is a clever child."

"Yes?"

"There is a good deal of Vernon, of my husband, in her."

"Is there?"

"Like him, she is very critical."

Mrs. Passenger sighed, and, thought Zouch, with good reason. They moved from flower-bed to flower-bed and from shrub to shrub, while Mrs. Passenger explained the garden and Zouch listened. He was beginning to feel that Fischbein was already very far away. In these peaceful surroundings it was difficult to believe that such a person as Fischbein could exist. Mrs. Passenger said:

"And the picture of Mary?"

"I have just begun a second one. The first was not a success."

"Do you find that she is difficult to paint?"

"She is not easy. She has beautiful features, of course, but her expression often changes."

"Yes," said Mrs. Passenger, "you are quite right. It often does."

She thought about Mary. The girl had not been looking well lately. She hoped that there was nothing wrong with her. She sometimes wished that she knew more about her daughters. Both of them seemed such a long way away from her and things were now so different from the days when she had been their age. She sighed again. It was time, of course, that Mary got married. One of these days the right man would come along. She took Zouch all round the garden, including the orchard, and when she left him it was nearly time for lunch. Zouch sat down on a stone seat and seeing a wasp crawling along the path he trod on it, half killing it. He watched its struggles until he heard the sound of the gong.

At the back of the Fox and Hounds there was a small garden which ran down to the canal. This garden was never used by the *habitués* of the saloon bar and it contained no amenities beyond a couple of green tables coated with dirt and a few iron garden chairs, one of which collapsed if any weight was put on it. There was also an arbour and some shrubs in pots. On the other side of the canal was a warehouse and blackened brick cottages with clothes hanging out to dry in their back yards.

"It looks as if it's going to keep fine for you," said Captain McGurk.

He watched Torquil hurrying about with bottles and glasses. The Orphans had been put in the arbour, which made a good background for them. Their organ had been wheeled in front of the arbour's entrance so that they were in this way partially imprisoned inside it. There had been some difficulty about getting them there at all because Captain McGurk was all against them and he only gave way because business was bad and he hoped to make at least a five-pound note out of Torquil's party. The Fox and Hounds had changed hands recently and had been bought up by a syndicate who had put in Captain McGurk and his wife to run it. Captain McGurk was an older and more successful Jasper. He had enjoyed less considerable social advantages than Jasper but he made up for this with the traditional virtues of his race. He always wore plus-fours and a school tie and had once appeared at a local fancy dress ball in a kilt. He and Jasper were great friends and used to spend a good many of their spare hours talking over what a high old time it had been possible to have on leave when the war had been in progress. Mrs. McGurk, who was also Scotch, had freckles and the thickest pair of ankles in the county. Betty Passenger had once said that people came in from miles round to see them, but as the Fox and Hounds was almost deserted except on market-days this was an exaggeration.

Torquil had arrived early and was preparing for his party by rearranging the garden chairs and helping to uncork some of the bottles that Captain McGurk had brought out into the garden with his own hands. Captain McGurk and his wife had been invited to the party as guests, and although Captain McGurk did not care for Torquil and thought him degenerate he saw no reason why this should debar him from having a drink at Torquil's expense, and besides, his wife was anxious to meet Mary Passenger, who had never before entered the Fox and Hounds. Torquil was dressed in a grey suit that was almost lilac in shade and although he was nervous about his duties as host he was also very excited and he rushed about giving orders and making suggestions and trying to make the Orphans understand what he wanted them to do. In this he was surprisingly successful. Although he was almost incapable of transacting any form of ordinary business such as buying a common object in a shop and paying for it without some immense and unforeseen difficulty arising, Torquil was consummately skilful in dealing with the Orphans, whom most people found not easy to manage. While he was doing this Jasper sat on the wall overlooking the canal and sampled the cocktails.

The guests, a small and select band, all arrived at the same moment. They consisted of Betty and Mary Passenger, Zouch, Joanna, the two Miss Brabys, daughters of the vicar, and Young Kittermaster. There was also to be present an Oxford friend of Torquil who lived about twenty miles dis-

tant, but he had already telephoned through to say that his
car had broken down *en route*. The Misses Braby were
twins who had shapeless faces on which the features seemed
to have been placed fortuitously without any attempt at
assembling them in such a way as to convey a significance.
They were very overwrought at finding themselves at a
cocktail-party and had kept the invitation a secret from
their father. Young Kittermaster, another of Jasper's
friends, was at Cambridge. He was tall, with very long
legs, and was always dressed in riding-breeches and suède
leggings. He had fair, rather sparse hair and thought himself a little like the Prince of Wales. He was called Young
Kittermaster because his father, who farmed on a fairly
large scale in the neighbourhood, was called Old Kittermaster. He was occasionally asked up to Passenger to
play tennis when there was a shortage of men. Like Captain McGurk he was not very keen on Torquil but he
had decided to put up with him during that afternoon for
the same reasons.

As they went through the lounge and out into the garden
Zouch heard Mary whisper to Betty:

"This is going to be appalling. We can't stay long."

Torquil came forward with a cocktail-shaker in his hand.
He put this down on one of the tables and shook hands
with his guests.

"Will you have a martini or a fosdick?" he said.

"What is a fosdick?"

"It's an invention of my own."

All of them chose a fosdick, Torquil's own concoction,
which was sweet and evidently quite strong. The Orphans
began to play the *Barcarolle*, the first tune in their reper-
toire. Everyone stood about at first rather awkwardly, sip-
ping their drinks and sometimes going down to the end
of the garden and looking at the canal like a stream of oil

slowly flowing past the houses. It was a pleasant evening, warm without being too hot, and later there would be one of the sunsets which Mrs. Brandon enjoyed so much.

"Well?" said Captain McGurk to Young Kittermaster. "How's farming?"

"Farming?" said Young Kittermaster, as if he had never heard the word before. He thought for some time, plunging his hands in the pockets of his riding-breeches and leaning against the wall. He concentrated for some minutes on his subject. Such a question could not be answered all at once. Then he shook his head slowly.

"We farmers are in a bad way," he said.

"Yes?" said Captain McGurk, as if this news seemed entirely beyond belief.

"That's it," said Young Kittermaster and took some more of his cocktail. "Not too good."

Jasper, who had sampled a good many of the mixtures before the guests had arrived, was looking more bright-eyed than usual and after a time he took Zouch by the arm and led him away from the others and down to the parapet of the canal. He was wearing bicycle clips on the ends of his trousers.

"Have a gasper, old man. There's something I want to ask you."

Zouch took one.

"Well?" he said.

"Look here, old boy," Jasper said, "I suppose you couldn't by any chance lend me five bob, could you?"

"No. I'm afraid I couldn't."

"That's all right. You didn't mind my asking you, did you?"

"Not a bit."

"That's all right then. No harm done. Daresay I'll find someone else."

"I hope so."

"I'll find someone else all right. Don't worry."

"All right, I won't."

"Don't you."

Zouch thought that the rest of the party looked as if they wouldn't be able to raise five bob between them, but as his only object in coming to the place was to see Joanna again he left Jasper and stood in a position where he could catch her attention when she finished the conversation that she was having with Mary. While he was waiting for a good moment to join in with them he was buttonholed by Mrs. McGurk, who said:

"How do you like our little town?"

"I think it's charming," Zouch said. "How do you?"

Mrs. McGurk said that she did not find it so nice as the country where she had been brought up and she gave Zouch a short account of her early life with a few thumbnail sketches of the outstanding characters among her relatives, and she was just coming on to her first meeting with her husband, which had been at Kirkcudbright during the war, when, seeing that Mary and Joanna seemed to have come to the end of all that they had to say to each other, Zouch muttered a few rather perfunctory words about how much he liked the Scotch and left Mrs. McGurk to Young Kittermaster, who had begun to smooth back his hair in an agitated way as if he were about to make a remark. Zouch reached Joanna's side.

"How are you?" he said.

"All right."

"Is that all?"

"What more do you expect?"

The cocktails were strong and after a sombre beginning the party showed signs of being a success. Joanna looked up at him and smiled. Zouch wondered how he could get her away for a few minutes from the rest of them. Before he could say any more Jasper came up and said:

"I heard a good one the other day——"

"Now then," said Captain McGurk. "Ladies present, you know."

"This one's all right. Not that sort at all. You see, there was a man and he went into a fried fish shop——"

"Listen," said Zouch to Joanna. "I want to speak to you."

He took her by the arm and tried to lead her away unobtrusively, but Jasper said:

"No, no, you mustn't go away. I want you to hear the story. It's a good one. He went into a fried fish shop and asked them what they'd got. He said had they got any salmon and the girl—the waitress, you know—said no they hadn't——"

"Here what's this?" said Betty. "I don't want to be out of this story."

"And so he said had they got any haddock and the girl said no, and he said had they got any cod——"

"Come on, Jasper, old man," said Captain McGurk, "get on with the yarn. We haven't got all the afternoon."

Mary was on the other side of the garden talking to the two Miss Brabys about the pageant. Mrs. McGurk, who had not been invited to take part in this spectacle, was listening with respectful interest. She drummed her fingers all the while against a table because the Orphans were now playing *Bluebells of Scotland*, an air which meant a good deal to her. Jasper said:

"Well, the waitress said they hadn't got any cod and so he said what had they got and she said they'd got some plaice and he said he'd have some. No, no, he said how much was plaice, and she said it was a shilling, and then he said he'd have some. And he said what vegetables were there? Were there Brussels sprouts? And she said there weren't Brussels sprouts and he said were there potatoes? And she said there weren't any potatoes and so he said what was there in the way of vegetables and——"

"Are you ready for another fosdick?" said Torquil, coming round with the cocktail-shaker.

"Torquil, you must hear this story," said Betty, slipping her hand through Torquil's arm. "Go on, Jasper."

"I want to speak to you some time away from all these people," said Zouch to Joanna under his breath.

Jasper took up another cocktail and hitched up his trousers. He said:

"So the man—no, I mean the girl, said well we've got some runner beans and the man said how much were they and the girl said they were sixpence and the man said that was O.K. by him and he'd have some runner beans with his fish and so the girl went off to get the fish——"

"But where did all this happen?" said Betty. "I didn't hear the beginning of the story."

"In a fried fish shop, of course," said Jasper. "Where did you expect? In the Ritz? And so the man ate the fish—no, no, I mean the girl——"

"What? Did the girl eat the fish?" said Captain McGurk, surprised that the story seemed about to take an unfamiliar turn.

"No, no," said Jasper. "Do keep quiet for a minute. The girl brought the fish and the beans and when she brought them there were only three beans and the man looked a bit surprised at this, but he ate the fish and he ate the beans and when he'd done he lit a cigarette and he asked for his bill and the girl——"

"But who was the girl?" Betty said. "Was he giving her dinner? Was she his *fiancée*?"

"Of course not," Jasper said. "He wasn't engaged to her

otherwise this wouldn't have happened. The girl was the
waitress. Anyway she brought the bill and it came to one-
and-six, and the man put down sixpence on the plate
and took his hat and began to walk out and the girl said
what did he mean by this because the bill came to one
and six and so the man said, '*Why, don't you know
that you don't get any plaice money when there are only
three runners?*' Neat, isn't it?"

There was a pause and then Young Kittermaster, who
had joined the group, said:

"Stout fellow."

"I haven't seen it," said Betty.

"Wait a moment," said Captain McGurk, "I'll explain
it, Miss Passenger—I mean duchess. I think I can tell it
better than that. You see a man went into a fried fish
shop——"

"But why did he?" said Betty. "That seems such an extraordinary thing to do."

"A man went into a fried fish shop," said Captain
McGurk, persevering, "and he sat down at one of the
tables——"

The Orphans had begun to play *The Bells of St.
Mary's*. Zouch touched Joanna's arm. The party was now
well started. Zouch separated Joanna from the rest of them
and by an adroit piece of manœuvring led her into a part
of the garden hidden by the corner of the house from
where the others stood.

"Shall we slip into the house for a second?"

"All right."

They went into the lounge of the hotel. Here for a short
time they could be alone together. The others would not
disturb them. Under the unaccustomed influence of cocktails the Misses Braby were shrieking with laughter,
Jasper and Captain McGurk had embarked on a flood

of stories, and even Mary was rather carried away by all these high spirits. Zouch and Joanna sat down on the leather settee in the middle of the lounge. Zouch took her hand. At that moment a man wearing a mackintosh and a bowler hat and carrying two suitcases came into the lounge and rang the bell. He took off his hat and rubbed his bald head with a handkerchief.

"Warm, isn't it?" he said.

"Real summer weather," said Zouch.

There was a broad low staircase in the middle of the lounge which led to the upper part of the house.

"Let's go up there," Zouch said. "We shall be out of the way."

"We can't very well go up there together."

"Why not? There's no reason why anyone should know that we have gone up there together. We might have gone up there separately."

"All right then."

They went up the stairs, and along the passage at the top of them there seemed to be nowhere to sit. The hotel was evidently not arranged for parties. One of the doors near them was open. Zouch looked in. It was a large bedroom, clearly unoccupied because the bed was not made up and there was a pile of blankets on it.

"What about in here?"

"Why not?"

They sat down on a small ottoman in the corner of the room. Zouch began to embark on the preliminaries of love-making. Joanna seemed not unprepared for this. She clung to him happily. The party was being a success.

All the while they could hear the organ playing in the garden outside, although both windows of the room were shut. There was a close smell in the room of linen and blankets and above the mantelpiece a coloured reproduction of *Her First Sermon*.

"We must go back now," Joanna said, after a while.

She was again a little frightened at the insistence of Zouch's love-making.

"Why?"

"They will notice that we have gone off together."

"Does that matter?"

"Of course it does."

It was soon after this remark that Zouch made a false step. He went too far. He was enjoying himself and in his enjoyment he forgot both his usual caution and his surroundings. He also forgot what Joanna was and how long he had known her. He overstepped the mark.

"What are you doing?" she said. "What are you doing?"

She struggled away from him and unexpectedly burst into tears.

"What's the matter? What on earth is wrong?"

"Go away. Don't touch me."

"But what is wrong? I'm so sorry if I've annoyed you."

But she only cried and cried. Zouch knew quite well what was wrong. He was conscious of having made a fool of himself. The question was how best to put matters right. He slipped his arm round her shoulder but she moved way from him. Zouch stroked his beard, wondering what would be the best thing to do, and watching her cry.

This situation might have lasted for some time if it had not been interrupted by something that was happening in the garden outside. The Orphans' organ, which was playing the opening bars of *Under the Double Eagle*, broke off suddenly. There was commotion and the voice of one of the Miss Brabys was heard to scream. Zouch went to the window and looked out. Something was happening in the garden. He could not see exactly what it was all about.

"Come on," he said, taking Joanna by the arm. "I'm sorry about that. Let's go down and see what is going on. They seem to be having a row."

Joanna sniffed and dabbed her eyes with her handkerchief but she allowed him to take her by the arm and lead her downstairs. The man in the mackintosh was still in the lounge. He was drinking a whisky and soda and he seemed unaware of the disturbance that was in progress outside. He looked surprised to see Zouch and Joanna again. They went past him and out into the garden, unnoticed by the rest of the party, all of whom were occupied by the scene which was taking place there. Something had gone wrong. The party was in an uproar. The Orphans had stopped playing their organ and Captain McGurk held one of them by the arm and was talking to him severely. The younger Miss Braby was in tears. Everyone else was talking at the same time except Betty Passenger, who leant against the parapet watching them and shaking with laughter.

"What has happened?" Zouch said.

Jasper took him aside and said behind his hand:

"Listen, old man, one of the Orphans made a pass at Gertrude Braby."

"Really?"

"He sure did."

"Why was it?"

"Torquil ought not to have given them the beer so soon. It went to their heads at once on a hot day like this. I believe one of them had a cocktail too, though I'm not sure. The eldest of them came out from behind the organ and went right up to her. We didn't know what he was going to do."

The Miss Braby who had been insulted was weeping copiously and her sister, who had been ignored, was preparing to do the same. In the fussing that was taking place no one noticed that Joanna's eyes were red and Joanna herself almost forgot about her troubles in the excitement of what was going on. The Orphan who had attempted to commit this act of violence was now quiet. He was sweating profusely and his yachting-cap had fallen on to the ground. His two brothers, speaking at the same time, tried to explain away his conduct in a stream of animal noises which they directed at Torquil.

As the worst seemed to be over Zouch thought that it would be a good moment to take charge of the situation.

"Now then," he said to the Orphan who had disgraced himself, "what is all this about?"

The Orphan said nothing. He was sitting on one of the most rickety of the green chairs and was rocking himself slowly backwards and forwards. Zouch said sternly to Torquil:

"You should not have allowed this to happen."

Captain McGurk and Young Kittermaster saw at once that Zouch's was the side to be on and they both glared at Torquil. Captain McGurk said:

"Yes, I say, look here, why did you?"

"Yes, I say!" said Young Kittermaster, smoothing back his hair furiously.

"Now then," said Betty, "don't be tiresome, all of you. You know quite well that it wasn't Torquil's fault. And anyway there's no great harm done, is there, Gertrude?"

Miss Braby could not speak for her sobs but she shook her head vigorously to show that she did not mind what had happened. Her sister was also crying a little by this time.

"No, of course there isn't," said Betty. "In fact it's made the party more amusing."

"I think we ought to be getting back now, don't you?" said Mary, who was standing beside her sister and who looked fairly angry.

"We'll go in a minute," said Betty. "I must just say two words to Torquil."

At that moment Jasper again took Zouch's arm and once more drew him away from the others and down towards the river. He said:

"By the way, old man, don't think me a bore, but what about that five bob that you were going to come across with? You nearly forgot about it with all this fuss going on."

"Me?"

"Yes."

"I wasn't going to lend you five shillings. I said that I couldn't."

"Oh come, look here, that's a bit steep, saying that now you're going to leave the party. You can't go back on what you said."

"I never said anything of the sort. You said that you were going to try someone else."

"Where the dickens could I try? I ask you?"

"I haven't the slightest idea. How should I know?"

"Oh, come on. Be a sport."

"Not a bit of it."

"You are a stinge."

"Maybe I am."

"I'll say you are."

"I don't care what you think."

"All right, don't get shirty."

"I don't want to discuss it further."

"Shurrup!"

Zouch walked away from Jasper. As he came up to the rest of them he was in time to hear Betty say to Joanna:

"But come up and stay the night at Passenger. Of course. You don't want to totter about two miles in fancy dress or go in a bus or something like that. Come and stay for a couple of nights. That will be far the easiest way."

He heard Joanna answer that she would like very much to stay at Passenger for the pageant. He tried to catch her eye but she looked away. Mary said:

"I really think we ought to be going back now. There are some people coming to dinner and you know how much father grumbles if we are late when there is anyone there."

They said good-bye to Torquil, who was in a highly nervous condition and full of apologies. The two better-behaved of the Orphans had so far recovered themselves as to play *Les Cloches de Corneville* but their brother's lack of restraint had spoiled the party and now everyone had begun to say that they must be getting home. Zouch hung about trying to get a look from Joanna but she avoided him and at last he gave it up and went off with Betty and Mary. On the way back Mary said:

"Betty, what made you ask Joanna Brandon to come and stay for the pageant? It will be very tiresome having her in the house all the time."

"She won't do any harm. I like the girl."

"Well, I don't."

"No, darling. I know you don't. But I couldn't help it. I suddenly felt like that. I expect it was the cocktails. Mother won't mind, will she?"

"No one minds. Only it will be rather a bore."

"I'll talk to her all the time. It broke my heart to think

E

of her coming by bus with her fancy dress in a suitcase or something like that."

"She could easily have got a lift from somebody."

"Well, perhaps she could, but there it is. I've asked her now and she has accepted, so I'm afraid you'll have to put up with her." And Betty added to Zouch: "Anyway, you don't mind, do you?"

"Why should I?"

"That's all right then."

Mary said: "You haven't apologised to us all yet for taking us to the beastly, beastly, beastly party we have just come from. It was far, far worse than ever I thought it would be."

Betty laughed. She said: "I didn't see much wrong with it except that the cocktails were too strong. I expect it will do Gertrude Braby all the good in the world to be nearly kissed by one of the Orphans."

When she considered her conduct in the privacy of her bedroom Joanna came to the same conclusion that Zouch had come to with regard to his own behaviour. She decided that she had made a fool of herself. She had stood on a dignity to which she liked to think that she attached no value. Her conduct had been of the very kind which in theory she most despised. She thought of her favourite heroine, Marie Bashkirtseff, and also about Madame Bovary which she had read in French with some difficulty. And then there was the whole of D. H. Lawrence's works. Besides she knew now that she was in love with Zouch. She had never been in love before. This was what she had been waiting for. And now that it had come she had perhaps ruined everything by her own primness. She began to cry again. It seemed the only thing to do.

Downstairs in the drawing-room Mrs. Brandon was talking to Dadds. She was on one of her favourite subjects and she was saying:

"Young people are so selfish nowadays. They think of nothing but enjoyment. They always want to be having a good time. In the old days it was different. It was thought right then to consider others. To do your duty. It wasn't just yourself all the time. But things are different now. But all the same I'm very glad that I was born when I was. I should not be happy if I were young now."

Mrs. Dadds sniffed to mark her agreement. She did not break in because she knew from experience, having heard Mrs. Brandon speak on other occasions of this contemporary problem, that her mistress had not yet finished all she had to say on this matter and that by waiting until she had run herself down she, Mrs. Dadds, would have a longer conversational innings herself. Mrs. Brandon said:

"We have our grey days, all of us, and our bright days too, and we must try to make the best of both and do what we can to smile through, even when the sky looks dark and things seem as if they won't come right. That's what I've learnt to do. I've had trials to bear as much as anyone I know. Look at my poor health. I'm debarred from living an active life. And yet I always look for the best in what the world offers. And if you do that you'll find that at last the sun breaks through the clouds."

Mrs. Dadds sucked her teeth in affirmation. Mentally she was preparing her own stuff.

"But young people won't see that," said Mrs. Brandon. "They think that life should be all sunshine. They want the silver lining without the clouds."

"That's all they want nowadays, pleasure," said Mrs. Dadds. "I used to tell my husband that. That was all he lived for, pleasure. I was saying to Miss Joanna the other day. I said she must remember that when she got married.

The men, they're all the same at heart. Every one of them."

"Yes, I suppose you're right. Miss Joanna will be getting married soon."

"Certain as winter following summer."

"She'll find a husband."

"All the same. The whole lot of them."

"One of these days," said Mrs. Brandon, "a handsome young prince will come along and take my little daughter away from me. He will steal her away and I shall be left all alone. But perhaps I shall be gone even before the handsome young prince comes riding past. I haven't been feeling at all well lately. I have had pains in my legs. Perhaps they are the beginning of the end."

"I got an earwig in my ear yesterday," said Mrs. Dadds, "I had to put a lighted match inside before I could get it out. It was something terrible. Terrible it was. Couldn't hear a sound. But it doesn't do any good to grumble. That's what I've always said and I'll go on saying to the end. That rotten husband of mine was a born grumbler. He wasn't happy when he wasn't grumbling, which was never."

"Grumbling has never done anyone any good and it never will. We must learn to face life as it comes."

"That's right."

"That's what young people nowadays won't do."

"Course they won't."

"It's a great pity."

Mrs. Dadds did not answer. She was thinking of her husband. Mrs. Brandon continued to expound her theories and she and Mrs. Dadds had quite a long talk together. Both of them felt better at the end of it and the pleasant way the time had passed was marred only by the discovery that Mrs. Dadds had forgotten about the things she had left in the oven, all of which were badly burnt. Joanna sitting in her bedroom also felt better. She had had a good cry and had thought things over. She went to her table and wrote a long letter to Zouch.

Torquil and Betty were alone in the drawing-room of the Fosdicks' house. Jasper was out playing golf with Young Kittermaster and Major Fosdick had gone off immediately after tea saying he had to tot up some accounts somewhere where he would not be disturbed. Mrs. Fosdick was away paying a call on someone. Betty, who had dropped in un-invited, sat on, talking to Torquil about the party.

"Then you don't think it was a failure?" Torquil said.

He sat curled up in a large arm-chair and peered nervously at Betty through his own cigarette smoke.

"A failure?" Betty said. "Why, if you'd seen some of the parties fail that I've seen fail you wouldn't be here to talk about them. You'd have died of it. I've seen failures in the way of parties that you couldn't even imagine. Why your party was a tremendous success. Parties aren't failures just because one of the band gets plastered and tries to kiss a guest. That means the party has been a success. It's been a bit different and gone with a swing. People want to talk about it after. They remember it among all the other parties they have been to. Goodness knows I'm not ambitious and I've never cared tuppence what happened at my own parties so long as I've enjoyed them myself, but I've known plenty of people who *have* wanted to get on, and they would never have minded a little thing like that."

Torquil said: "Of course I knew what Oxford parties were like but I didn't know that people went on feeling the same about that sort of thing."

"You've got a lot to learn," said Betty. "But you're a nice boy and I expect you'll learn it all in time."

"I've learnt a lot from you, Betty."

"I expect you have."

"A great deal. You have a wide experience of life."

"Oh, chase me!"

"I mean it."

"Come off it."

"You know, Betty, I think you are one of the few people who understand me. We have the same point of view."

Betty leaned across towards him. She said:

"Torquil, shall we get engaged?"

"Engaged?"

"Yes. I haven't been engaged for ages. Wouldn't it be rather fun?"

Torquil faltered. For a moment he felt as if he had been hit hard on the head. Getting married was one of the aspects of life which he had never even considered. There were hardly half a dozen women whom he could name as his friends. Apart from Betty there was Mary, who he always found difficult to talk to, and Joanna, who was easy. Then there were a few amorphous girls with whom he had sometimes danced at the local hunt ball and whose conversation was entirely about local matters. But here was Betty, who had lived dangerously and who was a duchess anyway, suggesting that they should get engaged. All his spirit of adventure was aroused. He said:

"Yes, Betty. Let's get engaged."

When he had said this he had no idea what he ought to do, but before he had had time to think about this he found that Betty had jumped up from her chair and, after kissing him, was lying back again and laughing a great deal. The situation seemed to him to be too important and even too ominous to laugh at but, taking his cue from her, he laughed a little himself.

"I never thought I should marry," he said, to steady himself.

But Betty only laughed. She said:

"Really, you know, my pet, you're quite the sweetest boy I've ever come across."

Zouch had decided that if he must indeed paint a portrait of Bianca it would be preferable, however unpleasant a tête-à-tête might be, to deal with her by himself rather than in the presence of her mother, or any of the rest of her relations. He had arranged her therefore at the end of the schoolroom in one of his stock settings and, although she strayed once or twice across the room, on the second occasion squeezing out on to the floor almost the whole of a tube of burnt umber, he found that she was less difficult to control by herself than when she was in the company of her nurse or family. She had been sitting still for nearly a minute and a half, holding her Mickey Mouse, but now she began to fidget again. She said:

"Do you like paint?"

"Yes," said Zouch, though the marks on the canvas belied his answer.

"Do you like gran'dad?"

"Yes. I like him too. Of course I do. Why, don't you?"

As a general principle he believed in acting with children as circumspectly as with adults. Bianca said:

"Gran'dad says he'll be glad when you get out of the house."

"Does he?" said Zouch, to whom the news came as no great surprise.

"Yes. He says he wouldn't trust you round the corner."

"Oh?"

"What would you do round the corner?"

"I might do a lot of things."

"What sort of things?"

"All sorts of things."

Bianca occupied herself for a short time with her own reflections. She frowned to herself, thinking evidently of the
gravity of Mr. Passenger's feelings with regard to Zouch.
Then she altered her position, trailing her Mickey Mouse
along the ground. She said:

"Granny doesn't like you either."

This information Zouch learnt with definite annoyance.
It was not so much that he minded whether or not Mrs.
Passenger felt well disposed towards him, although it would
have pleased him to have found that she did not share her
husband's unfriendly attitude. It was more the disappointment of knowing that all his conversations about the harvest
and the garden had been wasted. He had imagined that he
had been a success with her. For the moment he forgot his
discretion and was goaded into saying:

"And why not?"

"She says she doesn't know. She says there's just something about you that she doesn't like."

"Is that all?"

"She says it's just that. You're the sort of young man she
doesn't like. Mummy doesn't like you either. She says she'll
be glad when you're gone."

"Is there anyone in the house who does like me, Bianca?"

"Yes, Mary likes you. Mary is my aunt. Did you know
that Mary was my aunt?"

"Yes. I knew that," said Zouch, and had difficulty in
preventing himself from adding: "Worse luck."

"Mary says you're rather sweet. She gets angry when
Mummy says you're a tuft-hunter."

"Does she?"

"Yes. Mary gets very angry."

"I'm glad to know that."

"What is a tuft-hunter?"

"Someone who hunts tufts, I suppose."

"What is a tuft?"

"I don't know," said Zouch, rather bitterly.

"But how can you be a tuft-hunter if you don't know what a tuft is?"

"I can't, of course. I'm not one. Mary said I wasn't one, didn't she?"

"No. Mary said she didn't mind if you were."

"I see."

"Is gran'dad a tuft-hunter?"

"I shouldn't be surprised."

"Why wouldn't you be surprised?"

"Because—because——" Zouch was at a loss for words. He did not attempt to finish his speech. He was too angry.

"Shall I ask him?"

"Ask who, what?"

"Ask gran'dad if he's a tuft-hunter?"

"I shouldn't if I were you."

"Why not?"

"He might not like it."

"Don't people like being tuft-hunters?"

"Your grandfather wouldn't."

"Why not?"

"I don't know," said Zouch. "Perhaps he would. I don't really know anything about tuft-hunters, Bianca, and I think you must have made a mistake about the word altogether."

Bianca shook her head. She knew that she was right. She was prevented from saying more at that moment by her mother coming into the room, followed by Mary. She jumped up at once and ran towards them. Betty took both her hands, and said:

"Well, how's it getting on?"

All four of them looked at the picture, which had not yet reached an advanced stage in its presentation of Bianca owing to the difficulties of catching the sitter in any one position for more than a few seconds. There was a silence. Bianca spoke first. She said:

"Isn't it awful?"

"Bianca!" said Mary.

"It's not a bit like," Bianca said.

Betty said: "Well, I agree with Bianca that it isn't yet, but I'll give you the benefit of the doubt at present as to what it may look like when it is finished."

Zouch said: "Thanks awfully."

He did not care in the least what any of them thought, least of all Betty in the light of his recently acquired information as to the view she took of himself. The canvas was certainly in a mess at the moment. He did not need to be told about that. Mary said:

"I think it shows signs of being very good and I think that painting Bianca must be the most maddening thing in the whole world."

"Don't insult my daughter," Betty said.

"You ought to keep her in order."

"Anyway," said Zouch, "I've done enough for this morning. Let's go into the garden."

"Wait a moment," Mary said. "I must get some shoes on. Wait for me."

She touched Zouch on the arm and at the same time smiled at him in a way that showed her all at once to her best advantage, emphasising the freshness of appearance that he had noticed in her when he had first met her. Bianca said:

"I'll come with you, Mary."

"All right. Come along."

They went off together. Betty was left alone with Zouch. For a moment she looked after her daughter and sister as if

she were curious to know about something. Then she said
to Zouch:

"Look here, my little sister isn't falling for you, is she?"

"Falling for me? Really, please! Don't be quite so
absurd."

Zouch spoke quite irritably. During his stay at Passenger
he had found that Betty's way of talking grated increasingly
on his nerves. He had listened to conversations like hers for
most of his grown-up life and he had not come to Passenger
to be bored by the locutions of Montparnasse. Besides he
liked people to have a sense of their position, which Betty
seemed to lack entirely. When he thought about what
Bianca had told him he became even more annoyed. Except
for Mary the Passengers seemed to be a difficult, tiresome
family with their eccentricities and prejudices about ambition, which he himself had always imagined to be a virtue.

"Well, one never knows," said Betty. "Let's go down and
meet them in the hall."

They went downstairs, where Zouch found Joanna's
letter waiting for him. He noticed the postmark and slipped
it into his pocket to read in the privacy of his bedroom.

SIX

"You know, Mr. Zouch," said Mrs. Fosdick, "I think that Torquil will be a great success in life. I don't say that because he is my son. Far from it, although a great many of my family have distinguished themselves in one way or another I'll be telling you in my boastful Irish style. But Torquil has such a way with him. We thought he would probably do well in the Diplomatic. He has the manner, you know. And then they say that they are getting a very nice type of young man in the B.B.C. now, and besides there's no examination for that. Anyway whatever he does I'm sure he'll do well. He's so ambitious."

"I'm sure he will," said Zouch.

The pageant was coming to an end now and Zouch had been shuffling about all day in a pair of square-toed shoes with broad tin buckles on them. These shoes were several sizes too large for him and one of them was continually coming off. At the suggestion of Mr. Petal he was taking the part of Sir Peter Lely, a rôle which entailed no speaking nor acting and which had necessitated his presence in only a few of the tableaux. Mrs. Fosdick said:

"What career would you advise, Mr. Zouch?"

"What career?"

"For my son Torquil. I should be most interested to hear what you think."

"For Torquil? Let me see. What are his interests? Had you thought about interior decorating? There seem to be good openings in that business."

Before Mrs. Fosdick could answer, she was swept down the steps by a crowd of performers, who were being driven ahead by Mr. Petal, who kept on repeating:

"Ladies to the right, gentlemen to the left. Ladies to the right, gentlemen to the left. Ladies——"

In the confusion Zouch was left alone and he followed at the end of the crowd, who were on their way to watch the folk-dancing which was part of the day's entertainment. In his pocket he could feel Joanna's letter which he had read over dozens of times since he had first torn open the envelope. In spite of all that it said they had at present hardly spoken to each other, except for a moment when they had been left alone together just before the pageant had begun, when she had thrown herself into his arms and told him that he could do anything he liked with her. As the pageant was on the point of opening and the room in which they stood would at any moment be filled with people, this speech could only be taken as figurative, but Zouch was moved by the warmth with which she had said this and he remembered that she was staying in the house.

He looked round him at the garden which was crowded with little groups of people in fancy dress, most of whom had spent all day complaining about the discomfort of the clothes that they were wearing and telling each other that they could not imagine what had induced them to take part in the spectacle at all. The clothes themselves, especially those worn by the women, had not attained a high standard of historical accuracy, and, while the Kettleby girls were dressed in Italian cinquecento style, the Misses Braby had preferred to appear in some eighteen-fifty-ish frocks which they had discovered in an ottoman at the vicarage. Lord Chisleholm, a mild-looking man, who wore horn-rimmed spectacles, was taking the part of his ancestor the Lord

Chisleholm of the period, a noted rake, and he had chosen to wear a full-bottomed flowered coat over his ordinary hunting clothes, and many others also had used their discretion in matters of costume. Some excitement had been caused at the beginning of the day by Lady Anne Kettleby's dog-cart running away down the drive after the horse had been frightened by Dr. Smith's family, who were dressed as Yeomen of the Guard, but no one was hurt and apart from this everything had gone smoothly enough.

Mary and Betty had both sustained their rôles as Lady Castlemaine and Nell Gwyn with success and Captain Hudgins-Coot had made a very presentable Charles II. Mr. Passenger, who had decided after all to watch the pageant, had a fierce argument with him as to the way the Garter should be worn, which was settled only by the energy and consummate tact of Mr. Petal, only just in time : because Mr. Passenger had already lost his temper and was about to order Captain Hudgins-Coot out of his house. Mrs. Passenger had strayed away from the pageant itself early in the proceedings and spent the rest of the day looking for Capes in order to get him to repair the ravages made by mobs of people who now and then would be impelled by circumstances to walk across the flower-beds. But Capes was nowhere to be found. He had thought it a good opportunity to take his day off. Jasper had had too much cider-cup at lunch. There was no doubt about that. However, it suited the part he was playing and so no one minded much about that and Torquil also put up a creditable performance, without any artificial stimulation of this kind. The watching crowd included the McGurks, Mrs. Dadds, and two of the Orphans. Rumours of the bad behaviour of the eldest of them at Torquil's party had leaked out and accordingly he had been left at home in case the throng of people at the pageant might overexcite him. Young Kittermaster had stood at the top of the steps all day long, as a halberdier, and he looked quite faint with boredom.

But Zouch hardly noticed any of these people because he was thinking all the time about Joanna, who was herself thinking about him. He could see her, wearing a light blue farthingale, standing a long way away from him, behind Captain Hudgins-Coot. The pageant seemed as if it would go on for ever. While he was thinking he heard someone beside him say:

"They've dressed me up like a Christmas-tree."

Looking round he saw Major Fosdick, who, as General Monk, wore a feathered hat and gauntlets. The Major tapped his cuirass and said:

"It's absurd at my age. Dressing me up like this. I feel a regular figure of fun."

"My shoes don't fit," Zouch said.

"A regular figure of fun, I feel," said Major Fosdick with considerable pleasure. "It's a shame to dress me up. An old fellow like me."

He walked away from Zouch, chuckling a little to himself. Zouch went towards the folk-dancing and watched it for the rest of the afternoon. It was a long time before he had an opportunity of speaking again to Joanna. This came in the evening as he was going down to dinner. They met on the stairs.

"Do you mean what you said in your letter?" he said to her.

"Of course I do," she said. "I love you."

"To-night?"

"Yes," she said. "To-night."

He began to kiss her but they heard someone coming

along the passage so that they had to separate and go quietly downstairs to dinner.

The curtain had been drawn only half across the window and now it was light outside. Zouch had slept badly. He had cramp in one of his legs and, as he moved to stretch it out, he felt Joanna's arm resting on his shoulder. She was still asleep, twisted round with her face towards the pillow, lying curled up under the bed-clothes, almost all of which she had pulled over to her side. He disengaged himself from her and, getting out of the bed softly, he went across the room to the open window. He looked out of it towards the fields, at this hour unnaturally close to the house. The morning light brought them up just beyond the lawn. The grey, mysterious English fields. Small pockets of mist hung a short way above the ground and round the roots of the oaks in the park. Farther away the steamy mist grew thicker so that it filled the gap between the trees and hid the artificial water. But beyond, the atmosphere became clear again and the land rolled away upwards to the woods and cardboard hills. A sudden breath of cold air, intoxicatingly fresh, came into the room and he shivered and began to button up his pyjama coat which was open and which flapped around him. He looked at the time by Joanna's watch beside the bed and he knew that he must be getting back to his own room. His dressing-gown was on the floor. He picked it up and put it on, at the same time slipping his feet into his bedroom slippers. Then he leaned over and kissed Joanna lightly on the forehead. She stirred but did not wake. Zouch opened the door, trying to make as little noise as possible, but the hinge creaked menacingly. He set off along the passage in the direction of his own room. He was not feeling at all well.

The house was very quiet. Once he heard the voices of some of the servants as they went across the hall below the great staircase but upstairs there seemed to be no one about. He began to walk quicker but one of his slippers came off and, just as he had put it on again and was hurrying round the corner which led to the passage where his room was, he ran with great force into someone who was coming in the opposite direction. Their foreheads bumped together. The pain was intense. It was Marshall, the butler, whose agony and surprise caused him to make a loud sound, half-way between a grunt and a hiccup.

"Damn," said Zouch. "Damn."

He held his head.

"I'm sorry, sir."

"It wasn't your fault."

"I didn't think to meet anyone coming along just here at this time in the morning, sir."

"No, no. Naturally you didn't."

Marshall, who was in his shirt-sleeves and who had his tail-coat over his arm, now began to put the coat on. He had a large bump over his right eye. Zouch, who had had his head down, was bruised higher up on his forehead and less severely. Zouch said:

"I hope I didn't hurt you?"

"No, sir. No, sir. It is nothing much."

Zouch could feel his own bump rising all the time.

"You're sure?"

"Quite sure, sir."

"It looks as if it is going to be another lovely day."

"It does, sir. That's quite right."

"I thought I'd get up early and have a bath and then stroll round the garden before breakfast. That's the way to get an appetite."

"That's the way, sir."

"But now I've changed my mind and I think I'll go back to bed. Nothing like knowing what you want and doing it."

Zouch laughed. Marshall laughed too, but not heartily. There was a lack of conviction about his laughter. When they had finished laughing and Zouch was preparing to continue his journey to his room, Marshall gave an additional writhe to his shoulder to settle his coat on to his back, at the same time pulling down the tail of it, and said:

"And by the way, sir. There is a bathroom next door to your room, sir. I'm afraid you have had a long way to go every morning if you have been using the other one. I should have informed you."

Zouch said: "Yes, of course, the one next door to me is the one I use in the evening. But in the morning I like looking out of the window when I am drying myself and there is a better view from the window of the bathroom in the east wing. It looks across the park."

"Quite true, sir. Quite true."

"It is a particularly lovely view across the fields in the early morning. I expect you have often noticed it."

"It is a lovely view, sir. Certainly."

"It is part of my profession to look out for lovely views."

"Is that so, sir."

"It's my living, to record beauty."

"Indeed, sir."

As the prolonging of this conversation seemed to Zouch dangerously like waste of time and also because he was tired of standing in the passage, he smiled enigmatically at Marshall and walked on to his room. He got into bed and managed to sleep a little before it was time to go down to breakfast.

Joanna went back to her home the next day. She and

Zouch had no further opportunity of speaking to each other in private. People had remarked that she looked tired and she had said good-bye to them all as if she felt a little dazed, murmuring to Zouch that he was to come in and see her soon. No one's temper had improved since the pageant and Mary was in so bad a mood that Zouch had great difficulty in persuading her to come up to the schoolroom and sit for him, while he continued to paint one of the several portraits he had begun of her. All the time he was doing this she sat on the sofa looking sulky and fidgeting with the cushions that were propped up round her. It was as bad as painting Bianca. At last Zouch said:

"Oh, do keep still."

"I am keeping still."

"No. You've turned right round. You're in quite a different position from the one you were in before."

"I'm not."

"But you are."

"Oh, don't nag so. I don't particularly want you to do the beastly picture anyway."

She stood up, throwing one of the cushions into the corner of the room. Zouch put down his palette. This sort of behaviour was most unusual. Mary walked to the window. She stood there looking down on to the garden and twisting her handkerchief in her hands.

"What on earth is wrong, Mary?"

"Nothing."

"But what are you so angry about then?"

"I'm not angry. Do shut up."

"Don't you want me to go on with the picture?"

"No."

"But——"

Suddenly she began to cry. Zouch saw that a moment had come when he must act. In some way a crisis had been precipitated. It was all so sudden that he could not at once arrange precisely in his mind the inferences to be drawn from it but he became keenly aware that far-reaching issues were soon to be raised. He had known this, in a way, for some time. The idea had even crossed his mind when he had first met Mary. But Joanna and the events of the last few days had made him forget them, so that this reminder brought them back with redoubled force. Joanna had cried because he had made love to her too violently, and now Mary was crying because he had not made love to her violently enough. This must be remedied.

She tried to push him away, but not very seriously. He noticed that they were real tears. Scenes like this were becoming far too common in his life.

"Mary."

He kissed her, not too passionately in case he should frighten her, but with a great deal of care. He had become accustomed, during his stay at Passenger, to think of her in more detached terms than were usual to him when he was dealing with women and now he realised again how much as a woman she appealed to him. At last she pulled herself away from him and began to wipe her eyes with her handkerchief. Again he was reminded of the scene in the Fox and Hounds with Joanna.

As any further work was, for that afternoon, clearly out of the question, they sat down on the settee together. Mary began to speak. She told Zouch all about herself. She had never talked to anyone in that way before. She tried to put into words all the things she had begun to feel during the past few months. Zouch listened. When tea-time came he found that it had been one of those afternoons when he had become engaged. Afterwards he could never remember how exactly it had happened. All he was aware of was that his new life had now begun. The preliminary step had been taken. But caution would still be necessary for a long time to come and for by no means the first time in his life he said:

"But we'll tell nobody yet, will we?"

Mary hesitated. For a moment he thought that she was going to begin crying again. Then she thought better of it and said:

"All right. We won't tell anyone yet. I suppose you're right. It would be better not to tell anyone yet."

"I'm sure of it."

"Do you really think so?"

She seemed to be unconvinced on this point. Zouch said:

"Don't you think it would be better for you to prepare your family for the news after I am gone? I will go back to London as arranged and you can choose a good moment for breaking the news to them. Don't you think that will be better?"

Mary thought for a little time. Then she said:

"Yes. I think you are absolutely right. That will be far the best way. There's bound to be a bit of a fuss, but—but it's not as if——"

She was thinking about the dislike for Zouch which her parents had expressed and she meant to say that it was not as if she were financially dependent on them. Zouch understood this. He had made tactful enquiries as to how matters stood in that direction during the course of their talk and the information that Mary had given him was on the whole satisfactory. Mary said:

"Do you know what I thought about you?"

"No. What?"

"Do you know who I thought you were in love with?"

"Good heavens, who?"

"Joanna Brandon."

"But what could possibly have made you think that?"

"Oh, I don't know. You always seemed to be talking to her whenever you were in the same room with her. And then she *is* attractive, of course. I don't think she is particularly myself, but I know that other people do. I don't know why I thought it, but I did for some reason."

Zouch laughed reassuringly. He saw that he must begin at once to make all sorts of plans for his new life. Of *their* new life, he thought to himself.

"Do you think your parents will object very strongly?"

"Oh, they may a bit at first. You see they think——"

Again she did not quite know how to tell him what her parents thought about him. She decided to tackle the problem from its more picturesque angle, and said:

"You see they are not used to people wearing beards and that sort of thing. If you were a bit more ordinary——"

She made a tremendous effort to put her thoughts into words and said:

"Appearances mean such a lot to them. If you hunted and shot and that sort of thing, it would be all right."

"There is no reason why I should not do so."

Mary's words had come to Zouch as a great relief. If that was all that the Passengers objected to, things were not so bad. If they did not like conventional unconventionality they need not have it. No one would be better pleased to drop all that sort of thing than himself, provided that something better was offered in exchange. As for field sports he was entirely willing to play his part in them. After all he had a good constitution.

"Can you ride?" Mary said.

"Yes."

When younger, he had lived on a farm for some time and as far as he could remember horses presented no very serious difficulty. In any case the problem was not an immediate one. There would be time for him to give attention to this matter later, when he was back in London. Mary, to whom Zouch was still the embodiment of intellectual remoteness from that side of her life, was delighted. She saw at once that it was a splendid idea, and said :

"Why, of course, how marvellous. You can come again when hunting begins and we will fix you up with a horse. Father will be quite won over. That will make all the difference to his opinion of you."

"Then that is what I will do."

"How absolutely splendid!"

"Isn't it?"

In the heat of the moment his inexperience in this direction seemed a small thing compared to the importance of the goal at which he was aiming. He was aware that Mr. Passenger's dislike for him was founded on more solid foundations than the fact that he wore a beard or even the fact that he did not hunt, but he remembered that he was a superman and he saw no reason why he should not learn to do the things which were required of him with perfect ease. The will to power should teach him how to ride. He said :

"If I can come again in the autumn, I promise you that your parents shall have nothing to complain of."

"And then we shall be able to announce that we are engaged."

"What's engaged?" said a voice behind them.

It was Bianca. She had come into the room without either of them noticing her and she stood in her usual position, swinging on the handle and watching them.

"Why are you engaged?" she said.

Zouch went back to London at the beginning of the following week. The Passengers' car had driven off and he was standing in the waiting-room of the station, watching for his train to come in, when he saw that Jasper was also in the waiting-room, where he was occupied in reading the various notices of trains and posters, advocating Sunny Southern Sam or foreign travel, that were stuck on the walls. Zouch gathered his luggage together, as there was no sign of a porter, and went quickly towards the platform, but before he could pass the ticket collector Jasper turned round and caught sight of him. Zouch hurried on but he heard Jasper's voice behind him:

"Hi! Stop a bit, old man. Where are you off to?"

Jasper came panting up, his hands in his pockets.

"Going to leave us all of a sudden?"

"Yes. I have to go back to London. On business."

"Business? But I thought you said you were an artist?"

"Artists have business like everyone else."

"Oh, come on. Draw it mild. But I'm sorry you're going. Have the Passengers had enough of you?"

Zouch ignored this remark and engaged the ticket collector in conversation about the reasons for the lateness of his train. He tried to pretend to himself that Jasper was not there at all. If he took no notice of him, Jasper might go away. Jasper said:

"The London train starts from the other side. I'll carry some of your things across the bridge for you and wait and see you off. It's miserable having to start off by train without anybody to see you off. I know it is. I've done it. But I've nothing special to do at the moment and I'll be glad to do it for you."

As there seemed to be no way of preventing Jasper from doing this, Zouch allowed him to carry the heavier baggage and start off over the bridge while he himself paused to light a cigarette and buy an illustrated paper. It occurred to him that Jasper's presence might be turned to further account. When they had both reached the farther platform, he said:

"Have you seen anything of Miss Brandon lately?"

"What, Joanna?"

"Yes. I met her when she was staying with the Passengers. She seemed charming, I thought. I suggested that I should do a drawing of her some time but now I fear I shall be unable to do so. Will you tell her that I was called away rather unexpectedly, and unfortunately had no opportunity to see her again, and say that if she ever came to London I hope she will call upon me."

He felt that he was fairly safe in making the last suggestion and anyway even if anything so unlikely should happen as that Joanna should come to London she would do no great harm there. He hoped that she would be a sensible girl about the whole affair. Women could sometimes make this sort of thing so very painful. Besides there was a good deal at stake from his point of view. He said:

"Tell her how sorry I am."

"Right you are," said Jasper. "I'll tell her. That is I'll tell her if she'll see me."

"Why? I thought you saw a lot of her."

"She always says she's out now, it seems to me. Between you and me, I'm beginning to wonder whether I've got a dog's chance. What do you think? Shall I give it up?"

"Don't you," said Zouch. "You wait a day or two and then make a big effort. Wait about ten days or more and then go along when you're feeling in the mood. I shouldn't be surprised if you had a real success."

Jasper's eyes began to start out of his head. He produced three very old golf balls from his pocket and began to juggle with them.

"I say," he said. "Do you really think that?"

"I'm sure of it."

"What makes you think so?"

"I know about things like that."

"I say, you're a bit of a card, aren't you?"

"I certainly am."

The train, a local one stopping at all stations, steamed in slowly and Zouch found an empty compartment.

"There, put it in there," he said to Jasper, who still held the suitcase.

He climbed into the carriage and shut the door. Jasper said:

"Oh, and by the way, do you remember some time ago you said you'd be awfully kind and lend me five bob? I don't want to bother you but it would come in awfully useful if you could slip it across now."

Zouch felt that he could afford to be generous. His luck seemed to be in at the moment and he was in a magnanimous mood. He took half a crown from his pocket and held it through the window in the direction of Jasper.

"There you are," he said.

"I say. Thanks awfully. That's splendid of you. I'll let you have a postal order for it next week. What's your address?"

"Send it to Passenger Court," said Zouch, "and they will forward it on."

The train began to move out. Jasper waved and shouted something that sounded like "Tootle-oo." Zouch settled down in his corner and began to think things over. He was glad that he had met Jasper at the station. He was now absolved from any further obligation to get into touch with Joanna. He was conscious that a situation had arisen which called for the superman touch and he was satisfied that he was proving himself equal to it. At the same time he could not help regretting that, for the time being at least, Joanna was to pass out of his life. He put his feet on the seat in front of him and lay back, thinking about the future.

Jasper watched the train until it was out of sight. He had a slight obsession about railways and was often to be found hanging about the station, watching goods trains shunting or parties of men working on the line. As nothing much seemed to be going on that afternoon he left the station after a time and walked towards home. He decided to go round by the Brandons' house in case he might be able to catch a glimpse of Joanna. As he went he turned over in his mind the advice that Zouch had given to him about his love-affair. He was wondering whether he would act upon this advice and wait to see her for a day or two, or follow his own inclinations and try to see her then and there, when the door of the red-brick house opened and Joanna herself came out into the street. She was on her way to post a letter, and did not see him. She walked in the opposite direction, towards the post-box in the wall. Jasper shouted:

"Joanna! Hi, Joanna!"

She turned round.

"Hallo, Jasper."

Jasper trotted up to her.

"Haven't seen you for ages," he said.

"No."

"How are you?"

"Frightfully well."

Joanna was looking more lovely than he had ever known her look before. She had a higher colour than was usual with her and her eyes were very bright. She stood tapping the letter against her hand.

"What have you been doing?" she said.

"I've been up to the station," Jasper said. "Watching the trains. You can learn a lot up there. You ought to go up there more often. And I've got a message for you."

"For me?"

"Yes. From that chap Zouch who was staying at the Passengers'. I saw him off in the train back to London. He said he was called away unexpectedly and he wouldn't be able to see you again to do the picture of you or whatever it was he was going to do."

"He's gone away did you say?"

"Yes. He said if you were ever in London he'd like you to call on him but he didn't give me his address so I can't tell it to you. Perhaps you know it already. Anyway I don't expect you'll be going to London so it doesn't matter much."

"But he can't have gone."

Jasper looked puzzled. He said:

"Why not? I thought I'd told you. I've just seen him go. I watched the train go as far as the place where the line turns north. He didn't get out before it started, otherwise I should have seen him."

He was surprised at Joanna's agitation.

"Did you want to be painted very much?" he said.

"Be painted?"

"Yes. He said he was going to paint you and now he won't be able to."

"Oh, yes. Yes, I wanted to be painted very much."

"Oh, I say. What bad luck."

Joanna did not say anything. She went on playing with the envelope in her hand. Then suddenly she tore it up. Jasper was staggered.

"Why on earth did you do that, Joanna?" he said. "I thought you were just going to post that letter."

"I was."

"Then why have you torn it up?"

"I just thought all at once, that I wouldn't send it after all."

"You are an extraordinary girl. But you know some people are like that. They suddenly change their minds. Torquil is sometimes just like that. I've seen him do just that sort of thing."

Jasper chuckled.

"He's a funny chap, my brother," he said.

Joanna still did not speak. At last she crumpled up the pieces of the torn-up letter in her hand and said :

"I shall go back now."

"When are you coming along for a spot of badminton?"

"Well I can't for a day or two. I'm rather busy."

"But what on earth can you be busy at, Joanna? You're always complaining that there's nothing to do here and now you say you are so busy that you can't come in and play badminton. Any day next week would do."

"I can't tell you at the moment anyway. I don't know when I shall be free."

Jasper saw that something or other had gone wrong. He knew now that he had been a fool not to have followed Zouch's advice in avoiding Joanna for about a week, though how Zouch could have known what her mood would be at the moment was more than he could make out. He suddenly had a good idea.

"I tell you what, Joanna," he said. "You like reading, don't you? When you next come round to see us I'll lend you the family copy of *The Good Companions*. That is if you'll promise to take great care of it and not to turn down the corners of the pages, because father hates that."

SEVEN

Although it could not be said that Mr. Passenger took well the news of her engagement to Zouch, he was not so angry as Mary had expected that he would be. He was about as angry as he had been over the business of the Canadian soldier and their cook, which had taken place during the war and at a time when Mr. Passenger himself was on a diet and needed special care. He said, as he had said then, that it was all quite ridiculous and thoughtless and that they were clearly unsuited to each other, but he remembered the result of his opposition in the case of his elder daughter's marriage and so he expressed his disapproval in comparatively moderate terms. It was some time before Mrs. Passenger could believe the news at all, and, when eventually she was convinced the whole story was not a joke, she brushed it aside as a whim on the part of her daughter that in a short time she would get over. Betty would not give an opinion on the subject, neither to her parents nor her sister. When she was told, she merely laughed and said that she thought that marriage was in the air. It was decided that the engagement should be kept a secret and Mary agreed that she would tell no one about it.

"It is not as if you liked the same sort of things," said Mr. Passenger. "He is an artist and leads what is no doubt a very useful life if you care for that sort of thing. But you have always liked outdoor amusements. You should be married to someone who could come out hunting with you."

"But that's just what he will do," said Mary. "He's not a

158

bit like what you imagine him to be. He will come out hunting with me. I've asked him to come again in the autumn and said that you will mount him."

"Good Lord," said Mr. Passenger, taken by surprise for the moment, "does he ride?"

"He rides extremely well," said Mary, hoping that when the time came Zouch would not let her down. "The question is whether or not we've got a horse that it wouldn't be insulting to offer him."

"Really, Mary, don't be so absurd. There is not a hunter in the stable that any man would not be glad to ride. The question is whether I should be prepared to lend one of them to someone whom I know nothing about."

"What about Creditor? Do you suppose that anyone would be glad to ride him?"

"Creditor has his faults, I know. After all, he threw me twice and much more severely than he has ever thrown anyone else in the house. I admit Creditor has some very bad habits. But he has some very good points too and his pedigree is impeccable. Perhaps I shall decide to sell him one of these days. In the meantime he's a horse I'm glad to have in the stable."

"But you tried to sell him to Captain Hudgins-Coot and after a day out on him he said to someone that he'd never ridden such a horse in his life."

"Who did he say that to?"

"He told Young Kittermaster, who told Jasper Fosdick, who told Torquil, who told Betty, and I got it from Betty."

Mr. Passenger made a gesture with his hands indicative of extreme annoyance. He said :

"What do you suppose Hudgins-Coot knows about a horse? He rides that same rotten old mare of his year in year out. She must be about a hundred by this time.

Besides, although he makes a very satisfactory secretary from the point of view of getting the subscriptions in, which takes some doing in this neighbourhood, when we're out with the hounds he doesn't go a yard. Not a yard."

"But that's no reason why he shouldn't be right about Creditor."

"It is a reason. It is a very good reason. You know nothing about it."

Mary saw that she had made her father angry but the conversation had in this way moved sufficiently far from the subject of her engagement for her to allow the discussion to drop. She could reopen it at a more favourable moment. She said:

"Anyway, when Arthur comes here again in the autumn you will be able to see for yourself. You're only prejudiced against him because he wears a beard and he says that he's going to shave that off." She ended rather appealingly, "I'm sure you'll like him when you really get to know him"; and before her father could collect his thoughts from the remarks made about his horses she had left the room.

Mr. Passenger stood for a few minutes in front of the fireplace, staring at the mat. Then he took the back of an armchair and advanced across the room pushing it in front of him on its castors. He wheeled it to the window and sat down. He was doing a little heavy acting for the benefit of his wife. When he had sat there for some time without any comment from her he blew his nose, making a deep note to attract her attention. As she still did not speak he said:

"What do you think about all this?"

"It is difficult to know what to think, Vernon."

"You are not being very helpful."

Mrs. Passenger did not answer. Her husband said:

"The whole weight of these matters always falls on my shoulders. It is I who have to make the decisions and take the blame if they are unsuccessful. Now in the case of this young man, if I say that I will not have him in the house again you may be quite sure that by the end of the year Mary will be married to him. You know how obstinate both the girls are. They got it from you. If on the other hand he comes down here again in a few weeks' time it will look as if I condone the engagement."

"I know, Vernon. It is not easy. It is not easy at all."

"These are the problems I am faced with. Is it any wonder that my health is bad?"

"Perhaps when she sees him again she will change her mind. I fail to understand how she can possibly find him attractive. I think it is just an attack of nerves on her part."

"Nerves? Nerves?" said Mr. Passenger. "What does she want with nerves at her age? Now if I had an attack of nerves it would be different. And anyway I shouldn't do anything so stupid as that if I had."

"Have you any idea what would be the best thing to do, Vernon?"

"I think I know exactly what will be the best thing to do. I shall show no signs of my disapproval. He may come down here again and you may be sure that by the time Mary has seen enough of him she will no longer want to marry him. After all, hardly any marriages would take place if both parties saw enough of each other beforehand. As for his being able to ride, I don't believe a word of it. You may be quite sure that if he ever comes out he will do something in the hunting field that will certainly turn Mary against him. And I very much hope that you will keep your head in the matter. Don't whatever you do, become excited and be rude to him in front of Mary. That will have the very opposite effect to what we wish."

F

"I think, Vernon, that it is very much more likely that you will become excited and be rude to him than I shall."

Mr. Passenger hunched himself up in his chair and put his face in his hands. As Mrs. Passenger left the room she heard him groaning to himself.

Mrs. Dadds, who was telling a story about her chilblains, brought her narrative to a more or less satisfactory conclusion and paused to regain her breath. Joanna made a note on the slate of one or two more items that she would have to buy in the town that morning and ground the pencil on to the slate's surface so that it squeaked piercingly. Mrs. Dadds said:

"Mr. Dawkin up at the Court, he suffers something terrible from them. Sometimes he can't sleep at night."

"Mr. Dawkin?"

"He drives the motor."

"Oh, yes, he has them badly, does he?"

"In the autumn something terrible."

"How beastly for him."

Mrs. Dadds shook her head.

"There'll be doings up at the Court," she said, "now that the young lady is getting married."

"Getting married? Which of them?"

Joanna quite regretted having shown so little interest in the opening bouts of Mrs. Dadds's conversation. Now it appeared that she was about to hear a piece of real news. Perhaps Dadds was not so bad after all. Mrs. Dadds herself was conscious that she had made a hit and she did not propose to exhaust her news all at once. She said:

"Mr. Dawkin said that he knew it was bound to come."

"But which one is it?"

"There's nothing being said about it yet and they do say Mr. Passenger is very angry indeed. It was Miss Bianca who told Mr. Dawkin. That child is a regular pickle. You should just hear the things she says. And she looks at you in such an old-fashioned way all the time."

"But who is it who is engaged?"

"It's the younger of the two young ladies, so they say."

"Miss Mary?"

"It's her, Miss Joanna. That's what Miss Bianca told Mr. Dawkin. She went straight round to the garage and told him as soon as she knew. She told him all about it."

"Who has she got engaged to?"

"Miss Bianca thinks the world of Mr. Dawkin."

"But who is it?"

Joanna saw no reason why she should show any dignity in the matter of wanting to know. It was a subject in which she was thoroughly interested. There were several young men in the neighbourhood whose names had been mentioned at one time or another in connection with Mary. Usually they were young men whom Joanna herself did not know except by name or sight from having seen them at local functions but the subject remained an interesting one all the same. Mrs. Dadds said:

"I disremember the gentleman's name. But he came here once."

"But who can it have been? No one ever comes here except the Mr. Fosdicks and I'm sure it isn't one of them."

Mrs. Dadds made hypnotic passes with her hands immediately below her chin.

"Like this."

"What do you mean?"

"With a beard," Mrs. Dadds said.

"What?"

"Came here one afternoon."

"Oh?"

"Do you remember, Miss?"

"Yes. I know who you mean."

Although the news was very horrible indeed it seemed at the same time to be about things that were inexpressibly far away and in another life. She felt an absolutely helpless despair but it was not so much this that mattered as the fact that there seemed to be no place in her mind in which to put neatly away what she had been told. It was like an embarrassing parcel that had unexpectedly been handed to her in the street, something that jutted out and was impossible to conceal from other people. She snapped in two the slate pencil that she held in her hands.

"But I daresay you knew it all already, Miss Joanna," said Mrs. Dadds, "and that it's just the end of the story that I've been telling you."

"No, I didn't know anything about it as a matter of fact."

Mrs. Dadds said: "You're that sharp, Miss Joanna, that I'll be bound you guessed about it. And they say, Mr. Passenger hates the sight of the young man."

All this conversation had obviously to be cut short as soon as possible but not in a way that might make things worse by rousing any sort of suspicions. Mrs. Dadds said:

"Well, it's you that will be getting married next, Miss Joanna. I said that to Mr. Dawkin when he told me. I said and it won't be to some young hobbledehoy with a beard neither. We'll soon have you engaged. But you remember what I told you about husbands and their ways. Just you think of that when the time comes."

Joanna laughed miserably and said in what was left of her business voice:

"Then that finishes the list of things for to-day."

She drew a little line underneath the list with half of the broken pencil. Then all at once things seemed so awful that she left the kitchen in rather a hurry.

She went upstairs to her bedroom. She could do the shopping in the afternoon. She wondered whether this was called having your heart broken. Anyway it was very unpleasant. She wished that she could cry. She lay on the bed and found that later on in the morning she was able to. A short time after that it occurred to her that it was early closing day so that she had to go out and do the shopping after all.

Major Fosdick sat in his dressing-room with the door locked. He was wearing the sequin dress and was singing and muttering a little to himself. Lately he had become very careless about the rest of his household finding out about his eccentricities. He himself was conscious of his own carelessness and at times it worried him but he comforted himself with the thought that as long as he did not wander about the house there was no reason why he should not talk to himself in his own dressing-room, and, although one evening his wife had passed and spoken to him about it at dinner, she struck him as being irritable merely and not suspicious. The more disciplined side of his nature told him that he would soon be going too far but there was also something in him which made him enjoy these risks of discovery. The spirit of adventure, he thought to himself. That was what it was. He got up from his chair and, putting his book upon the table, he lifted up his skirts and executed a few dancing steps in the middle of the floor. When he was tired of doing this he took his comb and his buttonhook and tapped a little tune with them on the side of the dressing-table. He was still doing this when there was a knock on the door.

"Who is that?"

"Me, George."

It was Mrs. Fosdick.

"What on earth do you want?"

"Why are you making such a noise, George? I thought the ceiling was coming down."

"Making a noise? What nonsense! I have hardly moved from my chair since I have been here. Am I never allowed a few moments' peace? Why must you always disturb me when I have an interesting book to read? I know the house is small and that is why I sometimes wish to get away by myself. Is not that a sufficient reason? I cannot understand why I should be made to submit to this incessant bothering."

"But, George, the electric light was shaking as if it was going to come down."

"Piffle!"

"But, George, it was."

"Will you leave me in peace?"

"Were you trying to move the dressing-table? I have always thought that it would look better by the window."

"Well? And what if I was?"

Mrs. Fosdick went away. Major Fosdick's instincts told him that he was being unwise. He decided that he must pull himself together. He sat quietly in his chair for some time. Later on he took a pencil and an old exercise-book and began writing poems.

EIGHT

In November it was still warm and when they held the opening meet in the big meadow which lay to the west of Passenger Court the ground was sodden with the rain that had fallen in the weeks before. But the day was fine. There was a yellow light behind the clouds. Winter had not come yet, though there was a threat of it in the bareness of the trees and in the grey hedges. The meadow sloped up to the kitchen garden, where a bonfire was burning and the smoke from this swept towards the road, filling the air with the fumes of autumn. Away on the other side of the laurels down by the lake a haze hung like steam over the black water. A steady south wind was blowing.

Joanna had walked over from the town because everyone in the neighbourhood was to be seen at the opening meet even if they did not intend to follow the hounds. When she arrived there was already a line of cars parked a short way off the road and even one or two dog-carts. She found Betty, wearing gum-boots and smoking a cigarette, watching the people arrive. Betty herself had not hunted since before her marriage. She had never cared much for riding, but she liked going to meets if they were held at all near home. She usually managed an average of about two a week throughout the hunting season and once during a period of energy, when she owned a small car, she had attended nine in a fortnight. When she saw Joanna she threw away her cigarette, crimson at the butt from the red of her lips, and said :

"Come up to see the fun?"

"Yes."

"I'm glad my hunting days are over. I don't think I could find a horse strong enough to carry me now. How do you manage to keep so thin? Do you know some special treatment?"

Joanna laughed. She said:

"I don't know. I expect it must be unrequited love or something like that. There are the Fosdicks. How funny Torquil is looking to-day."

The Fosdicks, who were coming up the road at that moment, had hacked over from the town. Major Fosdick was on a venerable charger, which, in relation to other horses held a status comparable to that attained by his Ford among other cars. His sons were mounted on suitably whimsical hirelings. Jasper rode a rusty black cob, on either side of which his long legs stuck out ominously. Torquil was on a tall bay of some age, which moved jerkily, never failing to stumble over rabbit-holes or other obstacles, and Torquil, perched on top of it, seemed in spite of his bad seat to be one with it because of his own bony elbows and massive equine head. Both sons were in ratcatcher and Torquil wore a canary-coloured waistcoat. Major Fosdick himself was dressed in faded pink and his hat showed signs of having been beaten out quite flat on some past occasion and then straightened with care but without complete success. He was mumbling happily to himself. The opening meet was a landmark of some importance in his year. Betty said:

"You know, I really think Torquil is rather a dear. I don't know why, because he is very silly, but I just do."

"He looks like Don Quixote at the moment, doesn't he?"

"Poor lamb, I'm afraid he does. I wonder how long he will stay on that terrible animal."

While they were talking Jasper had begun to walk his horse to where they were standing. He reined in beside them and grinned while the cob tried to crop the grass.

"Hallo, Joanna," Jasper said.

"Hallo."

"What's he like, Jasper?" said Betty, slapping the cob on his fat quarters.

Jasper said: "I haven't ridden him before this year. Last winter he galloped well. Father took him out cubbing once and said he seemed all right, but of course he couldn't tell. He rushes his fences. Goes to them all doubled up and usually charges straight through the middle. Or else he refuses and you come off. Why don't you come out some time, Joanna?"

"I will when you present me with a three hundred guinea hunter."

"I wouldn't go out hunting again," said Betty, "if someone were to give me a horse that cost three thousand guineas. That's how I feel about riding. I'd sell it and buy gramophone records with the money."

Jasper was not listening. He leaned forward towards Joanna, who was standing on the side away from Betty, and said:

"May I come and have tea with you to-morrow, Joanna?"

"Mamma has not been in her best form lately."

"All right, you come and have tea with us. Most of the family will be out, I think. I've got some things I must talk to you about."

"Oh?"

"Do come."

"All right then. But you come to us. It doesn't really matter about mamma."

"May I?"

"Yes. I've said so."

As a mark of satisfaction Jasper rammed his bowler farther down over his ears. Joanna looked round at the meet. Nearly everyone seemed to have arrived by now. There was never a big field and to-day about thirty had turned up. They were better turned out than usual and, apart from the Fosdicks, there was hardly anyone she could see whose appearance was actually calculated to provoke a roar of laughter. Betty said:

"Here comes Mary."

Mary, who was riding side-saddle and who looked very neat in her habit, trotted across to them. She rode well and all the good points in her appearance were to be seen to their fullest advantage when she was on a horse.

"Hallo, Joanna," she said.

"Hallo, Mary."

"My goodness," said Betty, "I'm glad I'm on my flat feet. I wonder what sort of a day you're all going to have."

Mary said: "Father is in one of his rages this morning."

"What's wrong now?"

"Judd has just discovered that two of the hounds are sick and father says they are the best two hounds in the pack. He's furious."

"What nonsense. They're such a mouldy pack that there's nothing to choose between the lot of them."

"Don't be absurd," said Mary, and turning to Joanna she said:

"By the way, Arthur Zouch is coming to stay with us again some time this month. You must come and see him. You know he's a great admirer of yours. He wants to paint you some time."

"Oh, yes. I forgot to tell you," Betty said. "That he's coming to stay, I mean."

"Oh, is he?" said Joanna, laughing. "I'd like to see him again."

She felt all at once so odd inside that she wondered if she were going to be sick. She patted Jasper's cob on the nose and the horse tried to bite her. She dodged her hand away and said:

"Yes, I'd like to see him again very much."

Mary said: "He says in his letter that he has shaved off his beard."

"No? Has he really?"

"I don't think he will look nearly so distinguished."

"Neither do I."

"Still, it will be amusing to see him without it."

"Yes."

"Here's the Master," said Jasper, and swept off his hat, releasing his ears from under it so that they flew out on either side of his head in their accustomed high relief.

Mr. Passenger certainly seemed to be in a bad temper. He was red in the face and was riding his heavily built chestnut with a short rein and giving a series of nods and grunts while he listened to Captain Hudgins-Coot, the hunt secretary, who was riding beside him and who was evidently trying to explain away some appalling fiasco that had taken place. Joanna, who was still conscious of a drumming in her ears, saw Major Fosdick, bent on having a chat before they drew covert, head his horse towards this couple. She said:

"When did you say that Arthur Zouch was coming?"

She felt that it was stupid of her to return to the subject, but she could not prevent herself from doing so. Mary said:

"I don't know exactly. He didn't say in his letter. But it will be in the next week or so. I'll let you know and you must come up and see him again."

Mr. Passenger, looking pretty sour, came towards them. Captain Hudgins-Coot went off towards one of the Whips. Major Fosdick, who had not reached them, stopped for a moment in his tracks, unable to make up his mind which he would follow and talk to. Betty said:

"Hallo, Father. You're looking younger than ever this morning. What's made you so pleased?"

Mr. Passenger said: "I've just caught that damned nursery-maid of yours trying to offer Affable a sandwich. If that sort of thing happens again I warn you she will have to go. I won't have her in the house. I'll turn her out bag and baggage."

Betty said: "Who on earth is Affable? The new footman? Don't tell me she has fallen for him, Father. I simply don't believe it. He's got spots."

Mr. Passenger looked with attention at his elder daughter for several seconds. He appeared to be contemplating something really stinging in the way of a reply but for some reason he thought better of it and merely said:

"Affable is the soundest hound in the pack. I might almost say the only sound hound in the pack. Anyway, the incident has some importance as creating a precedent, so I hope you will impress Whatshername with the gravity of her attempted act."

"Oh, Lord. Affable is a hound, is he? I'm awfully sorry, Father. I'll tell her. She's terribly fond of animals and she probably thought that he looked under-nourished."

"Perhaps she did," Mr. Passenger said. "In future I hope she will not be betrayed into a similar indiscretion."

He turned his horse's head in the direction of the hounds but before he could get away he was buttonholed by Major Fosdick, who had arrived by this time at close range and who said:

"Thinking of drawing Lambert's Holt to-day, Master?"

"No," said Mr. Passenger, "I'm not," and nearly riding down the Major he moved off in the direction of the First Whip, followed by Mary.

"Is Bianca going out to-day?" Joanna said.

She felt she must talk to prevent herself from thinking that Zouch was coming so soon again.

Betty said: "No. She's got stomach-ache. She is always having it. I think she must have inherited it from me."

"Well," said Jasper, "I expect I ought to be barging along now. See you at tea to-morrow, Joanna. Good-bye, Betty. I wonder what sort of a run we are going to have?"

The hunt had begun to move off and the hounds were now flickering and undulating down the slope, followed by Mr. Passenger, with Major Fosdick, not to be put off so easily, a good second. They went through the gate and out on to the road. The rest of the hunt followed, roughly speaking in financial order, and a desultory cavalcade of children of varying ages, some of them mere infants, fought a sort of rearguard action, dressed in jockey-caps and perched on saddles of every conceivable shape, some the basket howdahs of donkeys on the beach, others of Spanish or Moorish pattern, recalling Mexico or the armies of the East. Among these walked or rode grooms, anxious men, trying to make the best of things. The horses clattered along the road and turned the corner so that after a few minutes all of them were out of sight behind the trees, except for one very pathetic child of indeterminate sex, who, suddenly taken ill, had wisely decided to turn back with its keeper.

"Let's go across the road and up the hill," said Betty. "We shall probably be able to see them all from there."

They went over the turf, now all cut up by the hoofs of the horses, the damp earth giving out a hissing sound round them while they walked through the gate and climbed through the brambles of the hedge. As the branches flew forward the leaves spattered their faces with drops of water. They began to plod up the hill. Others were doing the same because from the top it was possible to see for some miles between a cleft in the hills along which, more often than not, the local foxes would take flight.

"Wonderful thing for the figure, this," said Betty as they reached the crest and stood above the fields.

Joanna looked towards the country below them, divided into squares of green and brown by the hedges and an occasional stone wall. In the break between the high ground the sky above the horizon was marked with strips of light where the sun was drawing water. These broad rays stretched up to the gap in the clouds, which parted to receive them in the neat formality of a canvas background, an Assumption scene or baroque ceiling. The wind had got up a bit and was beginning to blow the trees about.

She saw the hunt bunched up by a covert at the foot of one of the downs, a favourite place of Mr. Passenger's, but more from obstinacy, because it was the sort of place where a fox ought to be, than because experience had shown it to be the sort of place where a fox was. Hounds began to draw. On the outskirts of the field, someone, perhaps Torquil—it was too far to see for certain—was having trouble with his horse. He was riding it round, bumpily, in circles, trying to quiet the animal. The rest of them stood about in little scarlet and black groups, looking like cavalry pickets. There was a pause during which the pack seemed to have disappeared, permanently among the trees and then, jerkily on the air, Betty and Joanna heard the horn. Betty said:

"Why, they've actually found something in there."

The fox had a good start, with the hounds some way behind and the rest of the hunt nowhere. Torquil—it was now clear that it was Torquil—led the field, because his mare with remarkable intuition had decided to run away with him at the precise moment of the find. The enormous

bay charged the first fence, a low one, loosely built up, and
went pounding on, taking it easy over some broken ground,
the rest of them catching him up one by one. It was evident
that the mare intended to negotiate the next hedge, which
was considerably higher and had no gaps in it, by the
method which had proved so successful at the previous one.
Torquil himself seemed prepared for something of the
sort and when the mare changed his mind and jumped,
he went into the air, swayed violently, and he could be
seen trotting across the next field, still mounted, but in
a position that would have enabled him to pick up a
handkerchief from the ground if there had been one there
and he had been so minded. Betty said:

"That was Torquil, wasn't it?"

"Yes."

"Why does he do it?"

"It is really very unwise of him."

Betty said: "Oh, I do hope he doesn't get hurt. You
know you mustn't tell anybody, but we're engaged. I
thought it would do him so much good. I do hope nothing awful has happened to him."

"You are engaged to Torquil?" said Joanna. For the
moment she forgot entirely about her own unhappiness at
the surprise of this news.

"Yes, but you really mustn't tell anyone. Of course it isn't
in a way frightfully serious, but at times I get so bored living
here. And then he is so sweet. You won't tell anyone, will
you?"

"No," said Joanna. "I won't tell anyone."

She thought it the most astonishing news she had ever
heard in her life. And yet, ridiculous as it was, it seemed
good news in contrast with the things that had happened to
herself.

The hunt was getting scattered now. They saw Jasper

come up, long after everyone else, clear the hedge at great speed, and canter on. He passed his brother, who had by this time re-established himself to some extent but continued only to trot. Jasper turned to shout something back at Torquil and rode on. A short way ahead Mary was trying to close a gate with her crop. Major Fosdick, who must have had views of his own on a short cut, was trotting along the road among the second horsemen. A few minutes later there was a check at the top of the hill.

"Heavens," said Betty, "what a temper father must be in by this time."

"Yes," said Joanna.

She was still watching the hunt, but she had begun to think of other things. The check was proving to be a long one and gradually the stragglers found their way back to the main body of the field. The hunt was too far off now to be able to distinguish individuals. Suddenly the sun came out from behind the cloud-banks and covered all one side of the hill-slopes with dull light. It would be just the day, thought Joanna, to be conducting a successful love-affair. Screening the match from the wind with her hands, Betty lit another cigarette. A long way away a man, who might have been Captain McGurk, standing on a stone wall by the road, began holloaing and waving his arms.

Some weeks later, in the hall at Passenger, Zouch stepped out of his overcoat, a new one in loud but neat checks, and let it fall into Marshall's arms. He rubbed his hands together and turned half round so that he might judge from out of the corner of his eye what effect the loss of his beard would have on the butler. But Marshall kept his eyes fixed demurely on the ground.

"How are you, Marshall?"

"Not too bad, sir. Thank you very much, sir."

"Cold weather."

"It is, sir."

"I suppose we must expect some cold weather now. Seasonable."

"That's it, sir. All right so long as it's dry."

"Then it's all right when it's dry."

"Yes, sir. Nice, cold, bright, dry, winter weather."

Marshall clenched his already tightly compressed lips at the thought of these almost ideal climatic conditions, and, glancing up from the floor for a second, gave out a glassy look. Then he turned and walked quickly up the hall as if he were trying to get away from Zouch in a hurry. Zouch pursued him, also at a smart pace, and entered the drawing-room at Marshall's heels, nearly colliding with his back as the butler stopped dead and announced :

"Mr. Zouch."

As he went over the threshold, for an interminable second, one of those shapeless entities torn out of the abyss of time, it struck Zouch how different his feelings had been on an earlier visit to this house. He rarely indulged in introspection, which he disapproved of from all points of view, but for once he allowed himself to dwell for this uncircumscribed period on the change that had taken place in himself. And it was not only his feelings. His whole body had altered so that it was as if he had stepped out of a shell or been born again. The house remained the same. The robust smell persisted. To him it was still a mausoleum comparatively comfortably furnished. But his own status in it was immeasurably altered. Already he was more than a guest. There would soon be a reserved place for him, he thought to himself with jocularity, in one of this catacomb's sarcophagi.

He found himself shaking hands with Mrs. Passenger, who received him more vaguely than ever before. When Zouch had worn a beard she had known that he was one of two possible men, but now that he was clean-shaved the choice was infinitely wider and, after her greeting, she added:

"I saw your sister in Bond Street when I was in London last week but she did not see me."

Zouch was startled for the moment because his sister had married a surgeon who lived in Tasmania, but he recovered himself almost at once and made an appropriate noise in his throat, implying that her appearance in Bond Street was no surprise to him. He moved on to Mary and squeezed her hand. She seemed delighted to see him again. When he had done shaking hands with her he went over to Betty, who said:

"Well, it's a colossal improvement. Simply colossal."

"You prefer it?"

"Every time."

"So do I," said Mary, "but I was too polite to say so at once."

Secretly she had hoped that no one would mention the disappearance of his beard so that she could discuss it with him when they were alone together. It was just like Betty to treat it as a joke. She herself thought it a great change for the better. It made Zouch look younger and at the same time cleaner. Some of her doubts about him—because she had developed a great many doubts when he had left the house—were set at rest. Things were going to be all right after all, she felt. They had written to each other regularly all the time that he had been away but both found difficulty in expressing themselves on paper, so that Mary had often begun to wonder whether she had done a very silly thing. She saw that, even if this was so, she could not break with him at once on account of saving her own face with her parents and her sister, and she had been worried on this account, but Zouch looked so improved and successful as he came into the room that the interest she had felt in him a few months earlier was greatly increased. Once more she began to visualise herself in the rather romantic position of a fashionable painter's wife.

"How's business?" said Betty.

"Brisk," Zouch said.

This was true. His luck was on the turn again and he had been working hard all the time since he had last been at Passenger and had managed to earn a respectable amount during that period, some of his sitters having actually paid him on the nail. He saw that Betty was displeased about his engagement. Mrs. Passenger, on the other hand, was unchanged in her attitude, and appeared to be unaware or entirely forgetful of it.

"I've been painting the Lazaruses," he said, "and Anne Kettleby, whom you introduced me to at the pageant."

"How awful it all was," said Mary. "You were too noble to take part in it as you did. I really don't know how we all stood it."

"How is everyone in the neighbourhood? The Fosdicks?"

Betty said: "Everyone's grand. We saw them all at the opening meet the other day. Joanna Brandon was there too, looking quite ravishing. She has definitely got better-looking since the summer. I told her you were coming here again and that she must come here and meet you."

"Oh, yes, I should like to see her again," said Zouch, a little dubiously. He made up his mind that if he ever got married to Mary he would insist that Betty saw as little of her sister as possible. She was an unpleasant woman and a dangerous influence. He hoped that Mary would not unexpectedly develop similar traits. Betty said:

"And, talking of hunting, I hear you are going to come out."

"Mary tells me that your father is going to be kind enough to mount me."

Betty said: "Oh, it isn't kindness with father. It's cruelty. Absolutely pathological, I can assure you."

Zouch laughed heartily, thinking that what Betty said was all too true.

"I haven't been on a horse for eighteen months," he said conversationally, and without any reference to actual fact.

Betty said: "I haven't for eighteen years and it will be eighteen centuries before I do again."

"But, dear," said Mrs. Passenger mildly, "you used to like your pony so much when you were a child."

"I know," said Betty, "I know. But look how I've ended up. I'm a warning to all girls who like animals."

Mrs. Passenger sighed, but it was evident that she agreed to some extent with what her daughter had said.

"How is Bianca?" asked Zouch.

"She's very well. I told her you were coming her again and she was delighted. She said you could do another picture of her."

"I shall look forward to it."

He wished that they would all go away and leave him alone with Mary, whom he had thought about a great deal and was by now really very fond of. He often contemplated the life that they would lead together. He had decided that there was going to be an unpretentious exclusiveness about it. It would be in a world from which people like Betty would be, by their very nature, shut out.

"How do you do?" said Mr. Passenger.

He had come into the room without Zouch noticing his entrance and now he stood above Zouch's chair looking at him.

"How do you do?" he said again, and held out his hand. He succeeded in getting a great deal of what he felt about Zouch into his voice.

"Did you have a good journey down?" he said, and taking the newspaper from where it was lying on the floor beside Betty he sat down in the corner of the room and began to read it. Mrs. Passenger said:

"What was the result of your talk with Major Fosdick, Vernon?"

From behind the newspaper Mr. Passenger said:

"What results could there be? Results can only come when two sane persons discuss a subject. I might as well try to convince an ape that he was wrong as talk to that old imbecile. Nothing that I could ever say could possibly have any effect on him. He shoots all my game, his wife is for ever bothering me about the thousand and one committees that she sits on, his eldest son does nothing but ride on my hounds, and as for that boy Torquil——"

Mr. Passenger stopped for a moment and put down his paper, trying to find words strong enough to express his opinion of Torquil Fosdick. Mrs. Passenger folded up the piece of work she had in her hand and looked across, a little hopelessly, at her husband. Then she rose and went out of the room. Betty said:

"Now, Father, you mustn't say anything against Torquil. I like him very much."

"You like him?"

"Of course I do."

Mr. Passenger said: "He's the worst of the lot."

"He isn't."

"He's the limit."

"What do you mean, the limit, Father?"

"You know perfectly well what I mean."

Betty said: "Well, if you think that, it won't please you to hear that he and I are engaged."

"Betty!" Mary said, and even Zouch was outraged by this piece of news.

"Oh?" said Mr. Passenger. "You're engaged, are you?"

"Yes," said Betty, "we're engaged."

She stretched out her legs in front of her and leaned back in her chair. She was evidently enjoying the situation. Mary said:

"But when did this happen? You never said anything about it."

"A month or two ago."

Mr. Passenger took the newspaper and shook it straight at each end. Then he folded it in two and again in four and continued to fold it until it was a small bulky packet. He put this under his arm and walked out of the room. Before he reached the door he said:

"It is unbelievable."

No one else said anything at all.

Major and Mrs. Fosdick were sitting in the drawing-room after lunch and Mrs. Fosdick was reading the *Morning Post*. The sky outside the window was grey. After a time Mrs. Fosdick laboriously tore a piece out of the middle of the front page of the paper and handed it to her husband, who received the fragment cautiously.

"What is it, Veronica?"

"Do you think, George, there would be room in the house for a German boy?"

"A German boy? In the house? What house? I never know what you are talking about, Veronica."

"In our house. Our home. Widemeadows."

Major Fosdick moved round the arm-chair he was sitting in, so that he could face his wife.

"Now why should you think we should want a German boy? As it is I find it far too expensive having that old beast coming to look at the garden three times a week. Not that he ever does a stroke of work. What would the boy do? Why a German? Sometimes, Veronica, I really wonder whether you are all there."

Major Fosdick, in his irritation, crumpled up the piece of paper his wife had given him and threw it on the floor.

"Not as a servant, George. A guest. A P.G. It told you all about him on the piece of paper I gave you. He wants to come and live in an English family. *Au pair*, you know. I was thinking of Torquil. If he knew German it might help him to get a job. He would go and live with the German boy's family."

This project for the bodily removal of Torquil made Major Fosdick pause; but he saw at once the risks which would be run if his wife's plans were put into execution. Although the German boy might be better than Torquil in certain respects, it would never do to have a stranger about the house. Besides there was always the remote possibility that he might be worse than Torquil. Major Fosdick said:

"I never heard such a thing. A P.G. indeed. I won't have anyone like that in my house. What next? And where are you going, dressed up like that?"

Mrs. Fosdick, who was wearing a hat and coat, said that she was going to pay a call that afternoon and proposed to use the Ford.

"Where is Jasper?"

"Playing golf with Young Kittermaster."

"He's always doing that."

"And sure don't they love it, the spalpeens."

"And Torquil?"

"He has gone into the town to consult Dr. Smith."

"Why?"

"He has boils."

"What, again?"

"And are you going to be at home all the afternoon, George? It is Dorcas's day out and I have told Cook that she can go over to Thrumpton St. Giles. Her sister lives there and she is expecting a little stranger some time this week."

"A what?"

"A baby, George."

"And so because of that I have to sit in the house all the afternoon."

"It would be safer not to leave it empty, wouldn't it now?"

"I was going up to North Copse."

"Couldn't you write some letters?"

Major Fosdick grunted, and after a time his wife went away in the car. On the whole he liked finding himself alone in the house. It gave him a delicious feeling of freedom and the knowledge that he could indulge in any vagaries he liked without the danger of discovery. At the same time he was aware that this sort of knowledge often made him act recklessly. He made up his mind that on this afternoon he would exercise great caution no matter what temptations there were to the contrary course.

He went up to his dressing-room and settled himself down in his sequin dress, and because it was cold, he wrapped round his shoulders the antimacassar from the top of one of the drawing-room chairs. Then he began to write in his exercise-book. He found that he was in the right mood for composition on that afternoon. He did this for some time, humming and singing to himself. He thought, with contempt, of his wife.

The days were short now and it would soon be dark. Major Fosdick looked up at last from his writing and glanced out of the window. For a time he watched the clouds scudding past. The flow of inspiration had stopped now and he put the exercise-book back into his drawer under his evening shirts. Then he got up and moved about the room, looking for the book he was reading—a recently published work on the breeding of retrievers. It was not on the dressing-table, not in the bookcase, nor on the mantelpiece. Major Fosdick swept about the room, his gown rustling round him as he walked. Then he remembered. He had been reading it the day before when he had been sitting in the drawing-room before tea. It was lying in the drawing-room on one of the occasional tables. Major Fosdick paused with his hand on the key of the door. It was a risk. Nothing could be easier than to change his clothes before going downstairs. He thought for a moment. Then he turned the key in the lock and went out into the passage.

Mr. Passenger was very angry. It was not so much that he minded whom Betty married as far as she herself was concerned, because he knew that it was a matter of sooner or later only, before she decided to marry someone again, more or less unacceptable to himself. But that she should pick upon the son of a man whom he disliked so much, and who had caused him so much annoyance as Major Fosdick had done, was going too far. If the marriage were to take place Major Fosdick would shoot not only the birds that came anywhere near North Copse, but there would also be no keeping him away from the Passenger coverts themselves. And, still worse, the Fosdick family would spend all their time in the house. It was a time to act, and act quickly.

After leaving the rest of them, he had hurried in his agitation into the library and here he sat down for a few minutes, having thrown down the newspaper on the floor and taken a cigar from the drawer in his desk. He lighted the cigar and after a time went out into the hall. There he found an overcoat and a hat. The hat was much too small for him and proved on examination to belong to Zouch, and the next hat he picked up turned out to be equally useless, an old felt belonging to Betty. Mr. Passenger seized a very old hunting bowler and, jamming it down on his head, went out of one of the doors at the back of the house towards the stable yard. Dawkin was standing in the middle of the yard, cleaning the car with a hose. Dawkin was whistling and did not see Mr. Passenger coming, so that dropping the hose suddenly, he allowed a stream of water to sweep across Mr. Passenger's feet. Mr. Passenger kept his temper. He said:

"I want the car at once."

"It's all over mud down here still, sir——"

"It doesn't matter. No, no. I don't want you. I will drive it myself."

Dawkin looked doubtful. Mr. Passenger was notoriously dangerous at the wheel. He stood in front of the car as if he were going to prevent Mr. Passenger from entering it by turning the hose on him again. Mr. Passenger disregarded him and climbed into the car and sat down. He put his foot on the self-starter. It buzzed, but nothing further happened.

"Why won't the self-starter work?"

"Shall I crank her up, sir?"

"Yes, yes. Take the handle."

Dawkin wound away at the handle. Mr. Passenger again began to light his cigar, which he had allowed to go out. The engine of the car remained silent.

"She doesn't seem to be firing at all, sir."

"Why not?"

"Can't say, sir."

"Try again. I'm in a hurry."

Dawkin tried again. Again he was unsuccessful.

"Damn! Damn! Damn!" said Mr. Passenger.

"Have you got the engine turned on, sir?"

"Have I——"

They switched the engine on, and after that the car started fairly easily. Mr. Passenger ground his teeth. He started with a jerk and drove out of the yard and down the drive, between the gaunt lime trees, and out on to the road. The surface was slippery and the car skidded as he turned out of the gates. Mr. Passenger accelerated to the utmost. The car gathered speed and in a few minutes they nearly touched thirty-eight. The telegraph poles flew by.

It was a grey afternoon. Autumn was turning to winter, Mr. Passenger thought as he drove along. It's what I'm doing too, he thought, and for the moment the poetry of this image relieved his feelings a little. He began to compose in his mind the speech that he would make to Major Fosdick. The great thing would be to keep his temper. He would try to shut out all other considerations from the discussion and confine himself—at first, anyway—to pointing out merely the disparity between Torquil's age and Betty's. He would not even stress the fact that Torquil had neither money nor a job. That might wound Major Fosdick's feelings. He would concentrate on the question of their ages and put it to him as man to man. The one subject to keep off was North Copse.

On the outskirts of the town he passed the Orphans, who were plodding along the road wheeling their organ in front of them. Saner than the Fosdick family, he thought, by a long chalk. He stopped the car and, getting out, passed between the chains in front of the Fosdicks' house. The front door was ajar but the inner door was closed, so that he could not see into the hall. Mr. Passenger rang the bell. He had prepared the opening sentences of his speech. He waited.

While he waited he thought about Major Fosdick. In his mind he conjured up a picture of Major Fosdick, standing before him wearing a check suit and looking at him with moist eyes with pouches under them like a bloodhound's. While he thought about it the vision rearranged itself into Major Fosdick dressed in jodhpurs and carrying a crop. The fellow was always dressed like the Old Squire in a melodrama, Mr. Passenger thought to himself with animosity. As nothing seemed to be happening and the afternoon was quickly getting colder, he rang again. Again he waited.

And then there was this business of his other daughter. What could she see in Zouch? He did not take that affair very seriously because he knew that she was a sensible girl and he was confident that the more she saw of Zouch the less inclined would she be to become his wife, but all the same it was a disturbing thing to happen. Mentally he compared himself to King Lear. A Lear without a Cordelia. What had he done, he wondered, that he should be visited with these things in his declining years.

Mr. Passenger rang the bell again and then, becoming tired of waiting and, judging at the same time that an unexpected entry might give an additional force to his attack, he opened the inner door and went into the hall. He took his hat off but he did not hang it up on one of the hooks of the umbrella-stand and, striding past the gnu's head, he made towards the door in front of him beyond which he could hear someone moving about. Before he had time to reach this door the person inside opened it and came out. Mr. Passenger was surprised to see in front of him a woman, smartly dressed in the fashion of some fifteen years before. He took a step forward. The figure began to retreat.

The hall was badly lighted and at first Mr. Passenger supposed that he was in the presence of Mrs. Fosdick. He braced himself against an effort on her part to reopen discussions on local committees. He was too angry to be at all embarrassed by an appearance of having been caught breaking into the house. He said:

"Oh, Mrs. Fosdick, how are you? I wonder whether I could have a word with your husband?"

As the supposed Mrs. Fosdick did not answer Mr. Passenger added: "I am afraid that I have behaved rather unceremoniously in coming into your house in this way but I rang several times and, as there was no answer, I imagined that the bell might be out of order. At Passenger the bells are always out of order and, although I am perpetually having the batteries seen to, I find often that the only way to get hold of any of my servants is to shout aloud or to do what is required myself. As the first alternative is highly objectionable I have often, perforce, to adopt the second, but there seems little reason to pay persons to wait upon one if there is no machinery for summoning them to one's presence."

As, at the end of this speech, Mrs. Fosdick still said nothing, Mr. Passenger looked at her more closely, and on doing this he realised at once that the person to whom he was talking was not Mrs. Fosdick, because Mrs. Fosdick could not possibly have grown a heavy grey moustache in the few days that had elapsed since Mr. Passenger had last seen her. And yet the face under the cherries of the wide picture hat seemed familiar. Far too familiar. All at once, in spite of the winter weather, Mr. Passenger became bathed in sweat. With brutal suddenness he was made aware of the fact that he was in one of those situations when it was necessary to keep his head. Major Fosdick, too, was clearly conscious that something was wrong, but for the moment he, like Mr. Passenger, seemed unable to hit upon a solution to the complexities of this meeting. They stood there looking at each other through the half-light. Then Major Fosdick said:

"I know what you have come about, Passenger."

He took off his picture hat with a sweep of his arm and held it by his side. Mr. Passenger waited. He had had a romantic friendship with a boy at school who had become in later life a Commissioner in Lunacy. It was things like this which made Mr. Passenger regret that he had taken so little trouble to keep up with his old acquaintances. Even the most superficial observations let fall over the dinner-table on the subject of handling the insane might have come in useful now. Major Fosdick said:

"You have come to talk about North Copse, haven't you, Passenger?"

When he had said this it was as if a great load had been taken off Mr. Passenger's mind. The feeling of relief was instantaneous. Although, only two minutes before, his head had been full of speeches that he was about to make on the subject of Betty's engagement to Torquil, these had been driven all clean away by the implications of what he saw before him and those two minutes had seemed an age while he tried to compose a few sentences that would ease the strain which he felt himself to be undergoing. Although

Major Fosdick had committed himself to acts which spoke far louder than any words could do, words were still necessary to bridge over the moments that both had still to spend in each other's company. Given his cue, Mr. Passenger was about to speak of North Copse, but before he could open his mouth Major Fosdick, leaning against the wall and allowing the arm with which he held his hat to swing backwards and forwards like a village maiden at a trysting gate, said:

"I have been thinking it over, Passenger, and I have decided that you have a just cause of complaint over North Copse. After all, I don't preserve the birds. It isn't altogether fair on you. Perhaps it isn't even cricket. But do you know what I have decided to do?"

"What have you decided to do?" Mr. Passenger said, wondering how long the nightmare was to continue.

Major Fosdick said: "I have decided to forgo the shooting at North Copse and to sub-let the place to you at a purely nominal rent. I shall give my solicitors instructions to arrange matters with your solicitors, if you will be kind enough to give me their address."

Mr. Passenger felt in his pocket and brought out a pencil and an envelope. He wrote the address of his solicitors on the back of the envelope. When he had written it he handed the envelope to Major Fosdick, who secreted it in the folds of his dress.

There was a pause. Mr. Passenger saw that Major Fosdick was watching him with his bloodshot eyes. He edged away slightly. There might be danger. Major Fosdick held out his hand.

"Good-bye," he said.

"Good-bye," said Mr. Passenger, taking the hand and shaking it. "It is most kind of you to have spoken as you have about North Copse."

When he had said this he turned away and, shutting the inner door behind him, he went out into the road. He got into the car and shut the door. For a few seconds he sat at the wheel, thinking, with his bowler hat tipped forward over his eyes. It was cold outside the house and he had no overcoat, but he did not notice this as he sat there. He was overcome with a sense of failure. He had not risen to the situation. As a superman he had let himself down. In this moment of emergency he had been thrown back on the old props of tradition and education and when he might have enjoyed a substantial revenge he had behaved with all the restraint in the world. He started up the car, turned and backed, and made off slowly in the direction of home. It had been a bad day.

Inside the house, Major Fosdick removed the sequin dress and, putting it over his arm, he went down into the kitchen. There he took a poker from the fender and opened the top of the range. Underneath, the coke was red and glowing. Major Fosdick folded the dress into as small a compass as possible and, crushing the hat round it, he thrust both of these objects in the opening. Then he went upstairs and fetched the exercise-books which contained his poems. He pressed these down with the poker on top of the hat and dress and, when all these things had begun to burn, he used the poker again to replace the lid. The fire began to roar inside the range. Major Fosdick listened for a minute or two. He shook his head. It was the end of a complete section of his life. He sighed and went upstairs to his bedroom, undressing there and getting into bed.

Mrs. Passenger put down her lorgnette on the edge of her writing-table. She looked up at her husband in surprise.

"Dressed as a woman?" she said.

"Dressed as a woman."

"But was this something to do with the pageant? Had he forgotten that it was over? Was it a joke?"

Mr. Passenger sat down on the sofa and rested his head on his hands.

"There was always something unbalanced about that man," he said.

"But what did you do?"

"What was there to do?"

"You might have called someone."

"What good would that have done? The rest of his family are as mad as he is himself."

"Anyway, one thing is certain. We cannot allow the children to go to the house in future. That is out of the question. They must be told at once."

"Certainly, certainly. But how can we prevent them?"

"You must warn them. Don't tell them what happened to you, but just explain that it would be better to see as little as possible of the Fosdicks."

"Do you suppose they would take any notice?" said Mr. Passenger. "Look what has happened as it is. But I forgot to tell you. Betty has got engaged to Torquil Fosdick. That was really what I went down there to talk about."

"Got engaged? Vernon! To Torquil Fosdick?"

Mrs. Passenger stood up. In her agitation she began to put on her gardening gloves which were lying on the table beside her. She said:

"But you must do something at once to put a stop to this. Without a moment's delay. Vernon, don't be dilatory about this, will you?"

"Don't worry me, dear. Please don't worry me. I have done all I can as it is. I have just told you what happened. How could I speak to him about the engagement at a

G

moment like that? Of course he must realise that it would be impossible after what has happened. As it was, he spoke of North Copse. He agreed that the situation there is really very unsatisfactory and so he will forgo his lease. He was very reasonable about that. I cannot complain at all. He is going to behave very handsomely."

"Vernon, I think you should have spoken about the engagement, since it was that which you really went down to see him about. He may take your not having mentioned it as a sign that you have no objection to its taking place. Did not that occur to you?"

"My dear, it is quite likely that he knows nothing about it yet. We may still be able to talk Betty out of it."

"We are already having quite enough worry with Mary."

"Don't speak of it."

"But what are you going to do about Major Fosdick?"

"What can I do about him? You ask such strange questions."

"Someone ought to be told. There is no knowing what he may do next. Something disgraceful. In public."

"I don't see that I can do anything. I don't really see that it is in any way my business. Except that of course, as you say, I shall certainly tell the children not to go to his house."

"Perhaps you are right. It is certainly the sort of thing that we do not want to get mixed up in."

"I always disliked that old fellow."

"You know I never cared for him myself, Vernon. Nor his wife."

"Now one realises how careful one has to be."

"One does indeed."

"In the circumstances there seems very little to do."

"Perhaps you are right."

"Then shall we agree to say no more about it?"

Mrs. Passenger nodded her head and taking off her gardening gloves, went on with her writing. Mr. Passenger felt nearer to his wife than he had done for years. He thought for a second what a wonderful thing sympathy was.

NINE

"They took him away," said Mrs. Dadds. "Jabbering something awful, he was. Mr. Dawkin was passing. It gave him a rare turn. Might have been one of the Orphans, he said."

Joanna listened to the story of Major Fosdick's mental collapse in silence. The narrative had already grown in volume considerably since the Major had been driven quietly away early one morning to a nursing home on the south coast. Mrs. Dadds said:

"Shouldn't wonder if he spent a year or two in a strait, poor gentleman. Treat him something terrible they will. Fair devils they are."

"A strait?"

"Strait-waistcoat, miss. They'll give him a padded cell."

"But he has only had a nervous breakdown. He hasn't gone to an asylum. He'll be back soon."

Mrs. Dadds shook her head and sniffed.

"Poor gentleman," she said. "And there goes that Mr. Jasper playing about on the golf course just as if nothing had happened. Hitting about as if nothing in the world was wrong. And all the time his own father in one of them things. You wouldn't believe it."

Joanna knelt down and buckled on Spot's collar. It was time to take the dogs for their walk. Mrs. Dadds, preparing to leave the room, caught one of her feet in Ranger and nearly fell down. Ranger growled and tried to snap at her ankle, missed it, and fell asleep again.

"Come on, dogs," said Joanna.

Mrs. Dadds, aggrieved and rubbing her leg, watched them leave the house. Then she went back to the kitchen, muttering to herself. It was going to be a dull afternoon, because Mrs. Brandon was asleep and there was no one to talk to.

Joanna took the dogs out of the town and across the fields. She was going on one of the several possible walks in the neighbourhood and one which would take her back to the other end of the town, bringing her home at the right time for tea. The ground was hard and there was mist about in the hollow places among the fields. Joanna walked along, planning out her life. On this subject she found it difficult to come to any satisfactory conclusions. As she went through a clump of trees she heard horse's hoofs coming along the track on the other side and she came out in the open at the same time as Zouch, riding one of the Passengers' hacks, reached the copse.

She recognised him at once, although he had shaved off his beard. There was something about his appearance that she knew she would never forget. Zouch was not so quick to see who it was standing among the trees. He had thought it wise to go out on a horse once or twice before riding to hounds, and, as Mary was in bed with a cold, he found it a good opportunity for escaping from the rest of the Passenger family.

"Hallo," said Joanna.

Zouch reined in his horse and lifted his hat. For a few seconds they looked at each other. Then Zouch dismounted and said:

"Hallo, Joanna. How are you?"

"I'm all right."

"You're looking very pretty."

"Am I?"

"You're looking charming."

He slipped his arm through the reins and, going towards her, he took her hands in his. She let him take them but he felt that her arms were hanging quite limply from her shoulders. He said:

"Aren't you glad to see me?"

The horse, bored at the sudden lack of supervision, butted him unexpectedly in the small of the back and made him stumble. Joanna laughed. She said:

"Yes, I am rather, as a matter of fact."

"Tell me what you have been doing."

As she did not speak Zouch said: "Well. What has been happening?"

"Nothing."

"Oh, surely something must have happened."

"Major Fosdick has had a nervous breakdown. Some people say he has gone off his head. Nothing else."

"I heard about that. But what have you been doing? Haven't you had any proposals or anything like that?"

"Oh, yes, Jasper proposed to me again yesterday."

"Did you accept him?"

"No."

Zouch said: "You know, Joanna, I'm not sure that you are not making a mistake. You see I am very fond of you and I have thought a good deal about it and really, you know, Jasper is not such a bad chap. I know he has his faults. After all most of us have. He is not any too bright. I mean he doesn't appreciate things as we do and all that, but there are far worse-hearted fellows than Jasper about. And after all, whatever one may think about him, he is a gentleman. You can't help seeing that as soon as you meet him. I'm not a snob. I hate that sort of thing and I have to be specially careful because as soon as an artist becomes a snob, well he's done for. He just can't go on. But you're not the sort of girl who can marry anybody.

You want someone who can understand you and I'm not sure you haven't found the right man in Jasper. Anyway think it over. It never does any harm to get one's ideas into order."

"You mean you think I ought to marry him?"

"You know, Joanna, I believe I do."

"Well, perhaps I will."

"I think you might do much worse."

"And how is your engagement going?"

"My engagement?"

"Yes. Aren't you engaged to Mary Passenger?"

"Well, yes, I am."

"Then how is it going?"

"It's going quite satisfactorily."

"Good."

"You sound very bitter, Joanna. Are you cross with me?"

"Why should I be?"

"I thought you sounded cross."

"Not in the least."

"From the way you spoke I thought that you were. You must come and see us when we are married. I expect you will come to London one of these days. You always wanted to, didn't you? We shall probably live most of the time in London. Of course I expect we shall come down here occasionally."

"Well, good-bye."

"Are you going?"

"Yes."

"Aren't you going to give me a kiss before you go?"

"Do you want me to?"

He took her hands again and kissed her on the cheek. She felt quite lifeless to him. It was like kissing a block of wood. He was disappointed and said:

"You know, Joanna, I shall always be very fond of you."

"Will you?"

"Always."

"That's splendid."

He turned to get on his horse and had one foot in the stirrup when Spot and Ranger began to quarrel under the animal's hoofs, so that Zouch was compelled to hop quickly for several yards while he tried to steady his mount, and he was already some way away from Joanna by the time he reached the saddle. He waved his hand to her and began to trot. Joanna called to the dogs and continued to walk along the track which led by a semicircular route back to the town.

The library at Passenger was a white panelled room with book-shelves along the walls and a bust of Pallas Athene over the mantelpiece. The Passengers had all gone to bed and Zouch remained there reading *The Economic Consequences of the Peace*, because he did not feel in the mood for sleep that evening and there was something matter-of-fact about this book which appealed to the overwhelmingly practical side of his nature. He had been reading for some time when he heard the loud tramping of someone coming along the corridor. It was the weary, heavy tread of someone who carried a weight that he wanted to get rid of as soon as possible. Zouch sat forward in his chair, wondering who it could be. The steps came nearer. He heard the person, whoever he was, pause at the far end of the library and put something down before he opened the door. Zouch watched across the shadows of the dimly lighted room and saw Marshall, the butler, advancing towards him, holding an oil-lamp in one hand and in the other a pair of highly polished top-boots. Zouch put down his book as the butler came across the carpet. For a few seconds they looked at each other in silence and then Marshall, without any warning, said with terrifying intensity:

"The master's boots."

"Are they?"

For a moment Zouch thought that Marshall was about to spit, such a look of distaste passed over his face, but instead of this he put the boots down on the floor and simply said:

"Not half."

It was clear that Marshall was in an unbending mood. He still held the lamp in one hand in a statuesque attitude, a male caryatid, reminding Zouch of the day when first he had seen him on his arrival at Passenger Court several months before. But now Marshall managed to show that underneath the plastic formality of his exterior he longed for conversation. Communion with another human being.

"Bright as silver, aren't they?"

"They are," Zouch said.

"That's how he must have them. Nothing else will do. If there was so much as a speck on them he'd bite your head off."

"I suppose so."

Marshall put down the lamp on an ormolu table and looked at Zouch as if he were wondering whether or not it would be safe to speak his mind. To encourage him to speak ill of his host and father-in-law designate, Zouch said:

"I expect he is rather short-tempered at times."

Marshall glanced round the room and then came a little closer to Zouch. Huskily, he said:

"He's the rummest old blighter I ever met and as for the missus, she doesn't know whether she's coming or going. And that Miss Betty is a proper chip of the old block. Miss Mary is the only one of the whole lot who hasn't got bats in the belfry."

All this was in such accord with what he himself thought that for the moment Zouch was at a loss for words with which to express his agreement and before he could reply Marshall had begun to speak again.

"And then there's that little Bianca," he said. "Who ever heard of a child brought up like that child is? Dragged up. That's all it is. She'll come into my pantry and say things you wouldn't believe. And then when you ask her where she heard words like that, she say she heard her mother say them. She's a proper little madam, that child is."

"She is very spoilt, certainly."

Marshall nodded his head.

"A proper little madam," he said again.

"Has Mr. Passenger always been like he is now?"

"He's been like it," said Marshall, "ever since I've been here and that's close on thirty-five years. But I don't stand too much of his talk. The master knows that. He knows just the amount I'll stand. He has to be careful. I don't expect I shall stay more than another eight years."

There was a pause. Marshall's manner suddenly changed. He said:

"They're difficult, the whole lot of them, sir. Very difficult."

He took the lamp from the table and, picking up the boots with his free hand, he went off down the length of the library. When he reached the farther door, he turned and said:

"You never know where you are."

"You are quite right."

"Good night, sir."

"Good night."

Marshall disappeared and Zouch could hear his footsteps echoing all over the house as he went up the stairs. Zouch turned back to the section on *Immediately Transferable Wealth* and read for a few minutes more, but Marshall had disturbed him and after a while he decided to go to bed.

Mary continued to stay in bed with her cold. Dr. Smith said that it was a touch of 'flu and advised her to take care about it, so that Zouch found himself without an ally in the house, and, as it was now more difficult to avoid the other occupants than it had been during the summer, he spent a good deal of his time alone in the schoolroom, playing about with various half-finished pictures, which he had brought with him. Mr. Passenger, who, although he would not have admitted it to himself, was curious to see Zouch in the hunting-field, had suggested once or twice that he should come out, but Zouch, hoping to make his début backed up by Mary, had always found some excuse. He was aware that every time he refused, it scored a point to Mr. Passenger's hand and so, after a day or two, when it became clear that Mary, who had a slight temperature, would not be riding again for a week or more, he agreed to hunt on the following day. He hoped that his clothes, which he had bought at a well-known second-hand shop, would prove to be all right.

"I'm putting you on Creditor," said Mr. Passenger at breakfast. "I think you will like him. Mary rode him a bit last season and found him quite satisfactory, although of course he isn't up to her own horse, The Carmelite. Still I think you'll like Creditor all right. He pulls a bit sometimes but he should be fairly steady under your weight and I haven't any doubt about your being able to handle him."

"It's kind of you to mount me at all," Zouch said. "But I hope he won't take a lot of managing because I haven't been on a horse for some time, until the other day, when I went out here."

This was not, strictly speaking, true, because he had taken the precaution of attending a riding-school in the suburbs of London for some little time, in preparation for the new life that he was about to lead. Still he thought it better to be on the safe side about such matters. He did not trust Mr. Passenger, who in this matter had the whip hand of him. Mr. Passenger said:

"Oh, old Creditor is all right. You won't have any trouble with him. I thought we might hack over to the meet. It is a very short way from here. Judd can brings the hounds along. We mustn't be late. You're more or less ready now, aren't you?"

Zouch said that he had only to put a few finishing touches to his stock and Mr. Passenger left the room, having mentioned the hour when they ought to start for the meet. To fill in the time Zouch helped himself to a whisky-and-soda, which he hoped would also steady his nerves which were unaccountably on edge that morning. He sat for a while reading the paper and then decided that he would go round to the stables to take a look at his mount. He had passed Creditor's loose box two or three days before but no impression of the horse remained in his mind.

In the yard he found the groom, a sombre man with a fearful cast in one eye, walking up and down a sixteen-hand chestnut with white stockings. The groom touched his cap when he saw Zouch and said:

"Morning, sir."

"Good morning."

"Believe you're riding this 'oss to-day, sir."

"Is he Creditor?"

" 'E is, sir."

"What's he like?" said Zouch, patting Creditor's neck.

"A nice little 'oss, sir," said the groom, implying by his tone that Zouch was going to be allowed to ride something very special in the way of a hunter, and adding as an after-thought: " 'E pulls a bit."

"Does he?"

"Just a bit, sir."

"I'll look out for it."

Creditor turned round his head and bared his teeth in Zouch's direction. The groom put his hand on the horse's nose and worked it up and down as if he were pumping water.

"Ah, 'e's a playful little rogue, 'e is," he said.

"I bet he is," said Zouch, thinking that he wasn't so little neither, and he went back into the house to have another spot of whisky. He had two while he was about it and then he went into the morning-room and read the paper again and smoked his pipe until it was time to start.

Mr. Passenger came into the morning-room after a time. He seemed to be in a better mood than was usual with him, and after looking out of the window for a few minutes, he said:

"How are you looking forward to it?"

"A great deal."

"I'm afraid there was a bit of a frost this morning but the ground should be all right by now."

Zouch glanced out through the window at the garden. The trees there were swaying about in the wind. It would be cold out of the house.

"I went and had a look at Creditor," he said.

"What did you think of him?"

"A very nice animal."

"He's not a bad little horse," said Mr. Passenger. "Not bad at all. I think you will like him."

A few minutes later they heard the sound of horses' hoofs on the gravel of the drive. Clop-clop, clop-clop, clop-clop. Zouch was conscious of a feeling inside himself of internal tightening. An inward contraction of the muscles that was not altogether pleasant. He was glad that he had taken the precaution of having a drink before starting.

"There they are," said Mr. Passenger, and stood up.

Zouch followed him out of the front door where the horses were waiting for them at the foot of the steps. The sudden cold of the winter air on top of the whisky made him feel all at once a little muzzy, but he walked quickly towards Creditor and, putting his foot in the stirrup, he hoisted himself up. He was relieved to find on arrival that he was facing the conventional direction. Now that he was in the saddle it was not so bad. He gathered up the reins.

"How about the leathers, sir?" said the diabolical-looking groom, slanting both his eyes upwards and at the same time swivelling round the left one so that it appeared as if it might be about to fly out of his head at a tangent.

"They seem all right," Zouch said.

"Not too short, sir?"

"No."

He lifted himself a little in his stirrups and in doing so dropped his crop. One of the grooms picked it up and handed it to him. Zouch rearranged the reins in his hands. He followed Mr. Passenger, who had already begun to walk his horse down the drive. Creditor broke into a trot and came up level. Then he tried to canter but Zouch jabbed at his mouth and held him in. They passed between the lime-trees and reached the lodge gates.

"There's still some frost," Mr. Passenger said, as they went out on to the road. "The scent won't be up to much to-day."

"No?"

"How do you feel on Creditor?"

"Splendid."

Mr. Passenger said: "Those leathers look to me a trifle short for you. If I were you I should lengthen them a bit when we get to the meet. It's rather severe for you having them as short as that."

"I will," Zouch said.

He did not propose to do anything of the sort in case he should lose one of his stirrups irretrievably, but he thought it safest in the circumstances to concur in order to prevent Mr. Passenger from insisting on his altering the strap there and then.

They rode on over the slippery macadam, between the bare fields that ended in a mist which hid the hills. There were not so many people on the road. It was cold and the horses slid on the surface of light frost. The wind hummed by them as they passed the telegraph poles. In the distance in front a large bus came suddenly out of the haze. It lumbered on towards them.

"These things are the curse of the roads," said Mr. Passenger.

"There seem a great many of them round here."

"Far too many. Keep an eye on Creditor. He hates buses."

They drew in a little to the side of the road. Zouch in front. The bus came rolling past. A cluster of putty-coloured faces looked out at them from behind glass. Zouch felt Creditor quivering under his weight. He tightened his hold on the reins. Creditor gave several quiet snorts. The bus passed on and Zouch relaxed his hold again. They walked on along the road. And then, quite suddenly, without any warning at all, Creditor was off.

They went some way before Zouch realised that he was being run away with, sliding all over the road, pounding down on the hard glass surface. Zouch tugged at the reins but it was no good. Creditor was well away. He galloped along, panting, between the telegraph poles, somehow keeping his feet.

Zouch began to bump about in the saddle. He managed to hold his seat and they passed over several inclines in the road without coming down. Along this part of the road there were a few cottages and a group of country people at the gate of one of these turned to watch him gallop past. It was soon after this that Creditor came down. He slid across a frozen puddle on a flat piece of the road by one of the cottages and went over. Zouch came off, landing on his head, losing his hat as he fell. He lay there crumpled up by the side of the hedge and his hat rolled over and over in the road until it dropped into the ditch. Creditor too, lay on the ground for a few seconds, kicking, and then somehow he managed to get up and walked unevenly along the road, catching his hoofs in the reins, which dragged along below his head. He tried to trot but after a time he gave this up. Where Zouch had fallen there was some blood on the frost of the road.

TEN

Although it was turning out to be a cold winter, the atmosphere was warm enough inside the saloon bar of the Fox and Hounds where Jasper Fosdick was talking to Captain McGurk. Jasper had slipped out after dinner to have a quick one before going to bed. He sometimes did this when he was feeling melancholy, or, alternatively, in unusually high spirits. He and Captain McGurk had been discussing the death of Zouch.

"Ah," said Jasper. "It was a rotten thing to happen."

Captain McGurk agreed that it was indeed. Jasper fumbled at the handle of his tankard and shook his head. Captain McGurk watched him suspiciously, wishing to goodness that he would push off home to bed.

"A rotten thing," said Jasper.

"And when are you getting spliced?" Captain McGurk said.

"The date's not fixed yet."

"Looking forward to it?"

"And how."

"And what?" said Captain McGurk.

"And how," said Jasper. "And how. It's an expression."

"What is?"

"And how."

Captain McGurk grunted. He changed the subject.

"How's your governor?" he said.

"Getting on nicely. Says he's very happy where he is and doesn't want to come back for a long time."

"He needed a rest."

"That's right. He did."

"Rotten thing to happen."

"Rotten."

Captain McGurk edged away. He had had enough of Jasper for that evening. Times were bad and he did not propose to have a round on the house. Besides he had been seeing too much of Jasper lately. Sometimes he thought it kept people out of the bar to have Jasper there. He said:

"I'll be back before closing time. Got some things to see to out at the back."

He went away and left Jasper in the bar, alone except for the couple who were sitting in the corner at one of the tables. These were a man and a girl. The girl, a squat little folk-woman, wore horn-rimmed spectacles and a beret and the man, whose face was notched and wrinkled like a badly carved gargoyle, had a black hat on his head. Jasper did not much like the look of them but he wanted someone to talk to and so he said:

"Nice and warm in here."

"To be sure it is," said the man in the black hat.

"Did you go to the meet to-day?"

"No," said the man. "I didn't. I don't approve of blood-sports. We neither of us do, do we, Hetty? We're just down for the week-end and doing some walking. We often come to this part of the country. We like it round here. But you've finished your poison, haven't you? What about joining us in a glass of the same?"

"Thanks," said Jasper. "I don't mind if I do. It keeps the cold out."

"Pretty raw weather we've been having."

"Bitter," said Jasper. "Plenty of frost about. It makes the road bad going. It led to a nasty accident the other day. A young fellow got killed. His horse went down on a slippery road and he broke his neck."

"Dear me."

"Top-hole rider I believe he was too. Couldn't do anything about it though. Might have happened to anyone."

"Somebody living round here, I suppose."

"No. Staying with some people. A chap called Zouch."

"Zouch? I know somebody called that. But it wouldn't be the same man. He'd never be on a horse."

"Well," said Jasper, who had decided to make the most of the story such as it was, "I knew this fellow very well. He was a fine chap. He liked me too. We'd have done anything for each other. And he was a damn' good man on a horse. Even now I don't quite know how it could have happened, but you know what a slippery road can be. The funny thing was that he was an artist. That always used to surprise me. That he should have been an artist and such a good rider."

"An artist? Called Zouch? It must be the same man. Did he wear a beard?"

"Well, he used to," Jasper admitted, "but he shaved it off lately. He looked much better with it off."

"Then it is the same man."

"Now fancy you knowing him too."

"My name is Fischbein," said the man wearing the black hat. "I'm a writer. I'm quite well known. I knew Zouch just about as well as you could know him and, now I come to think of it, I once met him near here when we were hiking. He said he was staying at Passenger Court, but of course I didn't believe that at the time. But after what you have told me I begin to wonder whether he wasn't speaking the truth. He couldn't have been on a horse otherwise, could he, Hetty?"

Hetty said that she did not think it likely that Zouch would be on a horse in any circumstances, but Fischbein said:

"No, it's Zouch all right. You remember we never knew what he would be up to next. He was a funny fellow. You never knew when he'd want to see you. Sometimes he'd cut up nasty, you know, and pretend he didn't know you. Well, he's dead now, is he? Poor old Zouch. But what you were saying about his being a good rider is all wrong. He wasn't that. You must have been thinking of someone else."

Jasper finished his beer and scratched his head. He said:

"Well, maybe I'm wrong about that. Yes, of course I'm wrong. He wouldn't have been a good rider, would he? It was silly of him to have gone out at all. I expect he just fell off, and that was the truth of the matter."

"Yes. That is more likely."

"One of these——" Jasper was going to say "Cockneys" but there was something about Fischbein that prevented him.

Fischbein said: "What did he want on a horse, anyway? No wonder he was killed."

"It was darn' silly of him."

"It was, wasn't it, Hetty?"

"Course it was," said Hetty.

Jasper said: "It beats me what the Passengers had him there for at all, unless he was painting a picture of the old man or something like that. You know they say that Mary Passenger—that's one of the daughters—nearly got engaged to him, but I don't believe that. She has got her head screwed on far too well to do that. If it was either of them I expect it was Betty. She's older and has made a mess of her life. I've made a mess of my life, too, you know. Couldn't help it. But I'll say one thing for Zouch. He did have a way with him with the girls."

"Zouch have a way with him with the girls," said Fischbein. "Not a bit of it. Don't you believe it. I don't say that there weren't a few mouldy little pieces hanging about the place at times, but he never had any success worth mentioning. Did he, Hetty?"

"No. Course he didn't," said Hetty, with feeling.

"He didn't?" Jasper said.

"Not on your sweet life."

Jasper took a piece of his moustache in each hand and separated it in the middle thoughtfully.

"No," he said. "I suppose he didn't. He certainly didn't have any success with the girls round here. Unless, of course, as I said before, he made a hit with Betty Passenger. But he always talked as if he knew a lot about them in London and I believed him."

"What are the girls like round here?" said Fischbein. "You don't mind my asking him that, do you, Hetty?"

"Course I don't," said Hetty. "I'd like to know myself."

Jasper screwed his face into a terrible contortion and winked. He said:

"They're pretty hot, some of them, but you mustn't ask me because I've got to be good now. I'm engaged. I'm going to be married soon. And what a girl she is, too. You should see her."

"What's she like?" said Hetty.

Before Jasper could tell her, Captain McGurk came back into the saloon bar. His look of disappointment on seeing that Jasper was still there changed to relief when he saw that Jasper had attached himself to Fischbein and Hetty. This made the prospect of drinks on the house agreeably remote. Captain McGurk said:

"It will be time soon and the bar will be closing, so as you're staying here you may like to take your drinks into the lounge."

He looked threateningly at Jasper, who said:

"You know this lady and gentleman knew Zouch quite well. I've been hearing a lot about him from them. You know he couldn't ride at all. He just fell off on the road and killed himself that way."

Captain McGurk was not much interested. He said: "What did you think happened to him?"

"I heard he was a crack rider."

"He was the chap with the beard, wasn't he?"

"Yes."

"Is it likely he'd have been a crack rider?" said Captain McGurk, witheringly. "With a beard?"

"No," said Jasper. "Of course not. It was my mistake. And all this talk of his about the girls was all rot too. They hated the sight of him."

"Well, of course they did," said Captain McGurk. "Ladies don't want a man to look like a blooming furze-bush."

"But he shaved it off later."

"I know he did," said Captain McGurk. "But he wasn't the sort of man that ladies like." And turning to Hetty, he added very archly:

"Was he now?"

Hetty bridled horribly.

"I'll say he wasn't," she said.

"This coma," said Mrs. Brandon, "is sometimes terrible." She lay on the sofa, on the counterpane and on the red and green roses, surrounded by magazines and books and poker-work tables. Spot and Ranger sat huddled together in front of the fire, dazed by the heat of the room. Mrs. Brandon looked more two-dimensional than ever. Her face had almost disappeared under the recklessly applied cosmetics. She fanned herself with the *Illustrated London News* of some months before. Mrs. Dadds stood opposite, as far away from the fire as possible. Mrs. Brandon said:

"Dr. Smith is a very poor doctor, I'm afraid. When he

was here this afternoon he practically told me there was nothing wrong with me. He said I must be careful about my heart but otherwise I was perfectly all right. I know one can't expect much in a small place like this but it is very unsatisfactory to have someone as unreliable as that to attend to you when you feel as I do all day long."

Mrs. Dadds did not answer but passed her hand unsteadily across her nose. Mrs. Brandon said:

"To-day I feel very weak. I shan't last much longer. I shall be gone soon. I don't expect I shall see another summer."

Mrs. Dadds said: "We're none of us getting any younger. What's more there's a great deal of sickness about at this time of year too, and there's Miss Joanna looking as white as chalk and just a few months ago she was the picture of health and never looked so well in all her life. And my pains have been something terrible. I haven't known how to go about my work. I've had to stop sometimes and sit down on a chair. There's something unhealthy about this town. That's what it is. It pulls you down. It made poor Major Fosdick go as he did. It wasn't any wonder."

"The poor child has certainly not been looking well lately. She is excited about her wedding, you know. After all it is the great moment in a woman's life. Ah, I shall never forget my own. Coming out of the church, under the arch of swords, and into the sunshine."

Mrs. Brandon shook her head and sighed and lay back again as if the effort of remembrance had been too much for her. She said:

"But Miss Joanna's father was a man in a million. There wasn't anyone in the world like him. If she could only remember him, I don't think she could ever bring herself to marry Mr. Jasper. Of course I haven't anything against Mr.

Jasper, and it is for her to choose, but he does sometimes seem to me rather an awkward young man. He has so little charm. That was what her father had. Charm. No one could resist him. He had only to look at a woman for her to fall in love with him."

Mrs. Dadds said: "Ah, when Miss Joanna gets married she'll begin to understand a thing or two. Marriage isn't all sitting about and reading a book. She'll have to learn that. Twelve years to-morrow I went to the funeral of that husband of mine and yet it seems only yesterday that I was married to him. I shan't forget that day in a hurry. *Day of Wrath! O day of mourning! See fulfilled the prophet's warning!* They played that and I shan't forget it if I live to be a thousand. I thought, 'You're getting your deserts, by now, my man.'"

Mrs. Brandon did not answer. She had ceased to fan herself with the *Illustrated London News* and now she lay back on the sofa, quite still. Her eyes remained open, but they stared in front of her at nothing in particular. Mrs. Dadds made preparations to leave the room. She was an unobservant woman and did not notice that her mistress was dead. She made a few more remarks about human nature, illustrating them from incidents from her late husband's career, and, as these called forth no response from Mrs. Brandon, she concluded that, as sometimes happened, Mrs. Brandon preferred sleep that afternoon to conversation. In such circumstances Mrs. Dadds decided to go back to the kitchen. She did not mind whether or not the replies of her listeners had reference to the subject which she wished to discuss, but if she talked, she liked answers of some kind. Talking to someone who was asleep was not good enough. It cheapened her. She went back to the kitchen in a rebellious mood.

The corpse of Mrs. Brandon lay on the sofa. Her mouth

was slightly open and she stared at the wall opposite, at a place just above the photograph, which stood in its wide silver frame on the top of the cottage piano, of her husband in uniform, wearing a cocked hat. After a time Ranger found the fire too hot and got up and shook himself. He went across the room to Mrs. Brandon and sniffed at her dress. Then he moved very slowly towards the door and scratched against it to be let out of the room. He did this for some time, until Spot, disturbed by the noise, came across the floor to join him. They both scratched for a bit but when the fire had burned low and the room became less hot they returned to their place on the rug. Outside, in the town, the Orphans' organ was playing *The Bells of St. Mary's.*

"How is she?" said Mr. Passenger.

He was sitting in the morning-room and spoke to Betty, who had arrived at that moment from upstairs, where she had been talking to Mary who was still in bed. Betty said:

"Oh, she is all right now. Of course 'flu always makes you feel rather rotten for a time, even when it's over. And then all that business was a shock. But she doesn't seem so bad. She has had a letter from the Kettlebys, asking her to go over there for Christmas."

"Is she going?"

"She seems to rather like the idea. It ought to be quite amusing. If Charles Kettleby isn't in one of his rough moods."

"Is Charles one of the sons?"

"Yes. He's rather too hearty."

"Old Kettleby was just the same," said Mr. Passenger. "I was at Magdalen with him. He was dreadful."

Betty said: "Oh, and Father, speaking of Oxford, I've had another chat with Torquil and we've decided not to get married after all. He thinks it would be better if he became a Roman Catholic and went into a monastery instead, and I'm not sure the poor sweet isn't right. He hasn't got a marrying face, you know."

"Goodness me, so that is what he is going to do."

"I expect it will be all for the best."

"There would be another massacre of St. Bartholomew to-morrow if they had their way."

"Oh, not Torquil. Of course he wouldn't."

Mr. Passenger said: "It has been a difficult year in many ways. Of course that accident was unfortunate and worry-ing, even though it may in other ways, although I don't want to appear callous, have made things easier. I think you have been very wise to drop the idea of your engagement, Betty. Very wise indeed. I congratulate you on your good sense. I felt sure that I could rely on you, but I was worried about other things at the time when you told me. And then, naturally, I was upset at Major Fosdick going off his head. I know we didn't get on particularly well together, but after all he was a neighbour and I had a very disquieting interview with him almost immediately before he was taken away to the home. I have said nothing about the details of it to anyone except your mother, and I shall continue to say nothing, but I can assure you that it was a disturbing experi-ence. And now on top of everything else comes the death of Mrs. Brandon. Of course I know that I had not seen her for a number of years. Perhaps I have been rather to blame on that score. Her husband was an old friend of mine and, although he was a man with terrible faults, I was prepared to overlook a great many of them on account of the fact that we had known each other for so many years. He made an unwise marriage. I should not have minded that if only his wife had been a little more adaptable. Mrs. Brandon was a very good-looking woman, too, when she was younger. Still the daughter came up here occasionally, so the two families did not lose touch with each other entirely, although I never thought that you and Mary got on very well with the girl. Personally I like Joanna. She reminded me of her father."

Betty said: "I hear that she is going to sell the house now and go to London."

"Go to London? What on earth does she suppose that she is going to do there?"

"The same as everyone else, I imagine."

"It seems a very unwise thing to do."

"What is the point of her staying here?"

Mr. Passenger was not listening. He went across the room and straightened one of the pictures. He stood back from it to see the effect of what he had done and then moved the frame in the other direction. He said:

"Even you must agree, Betty, that I have had a worrying time. With scarcely anything to show for it. Again I do not want to appear callous but I don't mind telling you that it is a great relief to me to have control of North Copse at last. I know that you do not take much interest in sport but I can assure you that it was annoying to have old Fosdick shooting all my birds. It was more than annoying. It was positively maddening."

"It drove him mad anyway."

"You should not joke about that sort of thing, Betty. That is one of the sides of you which I can never understand. You never seem to be serious."

"Your letters, sir."

It was Marshall. He held out the salver gingerly towards Mr. Passenger, who took up a handful of them, and began to tear open the envelopes. After a time, he said:

"Bills. Bills. Bills."

He threw the remainder of the letters, unopened, on his desk and left the room. Marshall put the salver on a table and knelt down to poke the fire. He looked profoundly gloomy. Betty read her correspondence, a few picture postcards with foreign stamps on them. She said:

"There don't seem to be any cigarettes in the box in the library, Marshall. Would you see that some are put there?"

Marshall raised his head. He said:

"Mr. Passenger said, when I told him that we had no more Virginian cigarettes in the house, Miss Betty——"

Marshall paused at the gravity of what he was about to say.

"Yes?"

"He said, miss, that"—Marshall cleared his throat—"that it would do you good to give up smoking for a day or two."

"Oh, he said that, did he?" said Betty. "Well, I suppose I shall have to have one of his cigars."

"Yes, miss."

"There is nothing else to do, is there?"

"No, miss."

"And, Marshall——"

"Yes, miss."

"You had better take the picture of Miss Mary off the easel in the old schoolroom and hide it somewhere. I see that Miss Bianca has painted a moustache on the face."

"Very good, miss."

Marshall disappeared hurriedly and Betty was left alone. She went to her father's desk to look for the cigar-box.

Anthony Powell

'Powell is very like a drug, the more compelling the more you read him.' *Sunday Times*

A Dance to the Music of Time

'The most remarkable feat of sustained fictional creation in our day.' *Guardian*

A Question of Upbringing
A Buyer's Market
The Acceptance World
At Lady Molly's
Casanova's Chinese Restaurant
The Kindly Ones
The Valley of Bones
The Soldier's Art
The Military Philosophers
Books Do Furnish a Room
Temporary Kings
Hearing Secret Harmonies

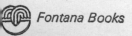 *Fontana Books*

Simone de Beauvoir

She Came to Stay
The passionately eloquent and ironic novel she wrote as an act of revenge against the woman who so nearly destroyed her life with the philosopher Sartre. 'A writer whose tears for her characters freeze as they drop.' *Sunday Times*

Les Belles Images
Her totally absorbing story of upper-class Parisian life. 'A brilliant sortie into Jet Set France.' *Daily Mirror*. 'As compulsively readable as it is profound, serious and disturbing.
Queen

The Mandarins
'A magnificent satire by the author of *The Second Sex*. *The Mandarins* gives us a brilliant survey of the post-war French intellectual . . . a dazzling panorama.' *New Statesman*. 'A superb document . . . a remarkable novel.' *Sunday Times*

The Woman Destroyed
'Immensely intelligent, basically passionless stories about the decay of passion. Simone de Beauvoir shares, with other women novelists, the ability to write about emotion in terms of direct experience . . . The middle-aged women at the centre of the three stories in *The Woman Destroyed* all suffer agonisingly the pains of growing older and of being betrayed by husbands and children.' *Sunday Times*

 Fontana Books

Fontana Russian Novels

Doctor Zhivago   Boris Pasternak
The world-famous novel of life in Russia during and after the
Revolution. 'Dr. Zhivago will, I believe, come to stand as one of
the great events of man's literary and moral history.' *New
Yorker.* 'One of the most profound descriptions of love in the
whole range of modern literature.' *Encounter*

The Master and Margarita   Mikhail Bulgakov
'The fantastic scenes are done with terrific verve and the nonsense
is sometimes reminiscent of Lewis Carroll . . . on another level,
Bulgakov's intentions are mystically serious. You need not
catch them all to appreciate his great imaginative power and
ingenuity.' *Sunday Times*

A Country Doctor's Notebook   Mikhail Bulgakov
'Based on his experiences as a young doctor in the chaotic years
of the Revolution. About 1000 miles from the lecture theatre and
30 miles from the nearest railway, he was faced with a bewildering
array of medical problems and the abysmal ignorance of the
Russian peasant.' *Observer.* 'Wryly funny – and fascinating.'
Sunday Times

The White Guard   Mikhail Bulgakov
'A powerful reverie . . . the city is so vivid to the eye that it is
the real hero of the book.' *V. S. Pritchett, New Statesman.*
'Set in Kiev in 1918 . . . the tumultuous atmosphere of the Ukrain-
ian capital in revolution and civil war is brilliantly evoked.' *Daily
Telegraph.* 'A beautiful novel.' *The Listener*

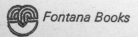 *Fontana Books*

Fontana Paperbacks

Fontana is a leading paperback publisher of fiction and non-fiction, with authors ranging from Alistair MacLean, Agatha Christie and Desmond Bagley to Solzhenitsyn and Pasternak, from Gerald Durrell and Joy Adamson to the famous Modern Masters series.

In addition to a wide-ranging collection of internationally popular writers of fiction, Fontana also has an outstanding reputation for history, natural history, military history, psychology, psychiatry, politics, economics, religion and the social sciences.

All Fontana books are available at your bookshop or newsagent; or can be ordered direct. Just fill in the form and list the titles you want.

FONTANA BOOKS, Cash Sales Department, G.P.O. Box 29, Douglas, Isle of Man, British Isles. Please send purchase price, plus 8p per book. Customers outside the U.K. send purchase price, plus 10p per book. Cheque, postal or money order. No currency.

NAME (Block letters)

ADDRESS

While every effort is made to keep prices low, it is sometimes necessary to increase prices on short notice. Fontana Books reserve the right to show new retail prices on covers which may differ from those previously advertised in the text or elsewhere.